Great Possessions

David Grayson

Contents

CHAPTER I THE WELL-FLAVOURED EARTH..7

CHAPTER II OF GOOD AND EVIL ODOURS...15

CHAPTER III FOLLOW YOUR NOSE! 19

CHAPTER IV THE GREEN PEOPLE...28

CHAPTER V PLACES OF RETIREMENT 35

CHAPTER VI +NO TRESPASS+ 39

CHAPTER VII LOOK AT THE WORLD!..46

CHAPTER VIII A GOOD APPLE..50

CHAPTER IX I GO TO THE CITY..57

CHAPTER X THE OLD STONE MASON 65

CHAPTER XI AN AUCTION OF ANTIQUES...71

CHAPTER XII A WOMAN OF FORTY-FIVE 81

CHAPTER XIII HIS MAJESTY--BILL RICHARDS...91

CHAPTER XIV ON LIVING IN THE COUNTRY..99

GREAT POSSESSIONS

BY

David Grayson

CHAPTER I
THE WELL-FLAVOURED EARTH

"Sweet as Eden is the air
  And Eden-sweet the ray.
No Paradise is lost for them
Who foot by branching root and stem,
And lightly with the woodland share
  The change of night and day."

For these many years, since I have lived here in the country, I have had it in my mind to write something about the odour and taste of this well-flavoured earth. The fact is, both the sense of smell and the sense of taste; have been shabbily treated in the amiable rivalry of the senses. Sight and hearing have been the swift and nimble brothers, and sight especially, the tricky Jacob of the family, is keen upon the business of seizing the entire inheritance, while smell, like hairy Esau, comes late to the blessing, hungry from the hills, and willing to trade its inheritance for a mess of pottage.

I have always had a kind of errant love for the improvident and adventurous Esaus of the Earth. I think they smell a wilder fragrance than I do, and taste sweeter things, and I have thought, therefore, of beginning a kind of fragrant autobiography, a chronicle of all the good odours and flavours that ever I have had in my life.

As I grow older, a curious feeling comes often to me in the spring, as it comes this spring more poignantly than ever before, a sense of the temporariness of all things, the swiftness of life, the sadness of a beauty that vanishes so soon, and I long to lay hold upon it as it passes by all the handles that I can. I would not only see it and hear it, but I would smell it and taste it and touch it, and all with a new kind of intensity and eagerness.

Harriet says I get more pleasure out of the smell of my supper than I get out of the supper itself.

"I never need to ring for you," says she, "but only open the kitchen door. In a few minutes I'll see you straighten up, lift your head, sniff a little, and come straight for the house."

"The odour of your suppers, Harriet," I said, "after a day in the fields, would lure a man out of purgatory."

My father before me had a singularly keen nose. I remember well when I was a boy and drove with him in the wild North Country, often through miles of unbroken forest, how he would sometimes break a long silence, lift his head with sudden awareness, and say to me:

"David, I smell open fields."

In a few minutes we were sure to come to a settler's cabin, a log barn, or a clearing. Among the free odours of the forest he had caught, afar off, the common odours of the work of man.

When we were tramping or surveying in that country, I have seen him stop suddenly, draw in a long breath, and remark:

"Marshes," or, "A stream yonder."

Part of this strange keenness of sense, often noted by those who knew that sturdy old cavalryman, may have been based, as so many of our talents are, upon a defect. My father gave all the sweet sounds of the world, the voices of his sons, the songs of his daughters, to help free the Southern slaves. He was deaf.

It is well known that when one sense is defective the others fly to the rescue, and my father's singular development of the sense of smell may have been due in part to this defect, though I believe it to have been, to a far larger degree, a native gift. Me had a downright good nose. All his life long he enjoyed with more than ordinary keenness the odour of flowers, and would often pick a sprig of wild rose and carry it along with him in his hand, sniffing at it from time to time, and he loved the lilac, as I do after him. To ill odours he was not less sensitive, and was impatient of rats in the barn, and could smell them, among other odours, the moment the door was opened. He always had a peculiar sensitiveness to the presence of animals, as of dogs, cats, muskrats, cattle, horses, and the like, and would speak of them long before he had seen them or could know that they were about.

I recall once on a wild Northern lake, when we were working along the shore in a boat, how he stopped suddenly and exclaimed:

"David, do you hear anything?"--for I, a boy, was ears for him in those wilderness places.

"No, Father. What is it?"

"Indians."

And, sure enough, in a short time I heard the barking of their dogs and we came soon upon their camp, where, I remember, they were drying deer meat upon a frame of poplar poles over an open fire. He told me that the smoky smell of the Indians, tanned buckskin, parched wild rice, and the like, were odours that carried far and could not be mistaken.

My father had a big, hooked nose with long, narrow nostrils, I suppose that this has really nothing to do with the matter, although I have come, after these many years, to look with a curious interest upon people's noses, since I know what a vehicle of delight they often are. My own nose is nothing to speak of, good enough as noses go--but I think I inherited from my father something of the power of enjoyment he had from that sense, though I can never hope to become the accomplished smeller he was.

I am moved to begin this chronicle because of my joy this morning early--a May morning!--just after sunrise, when the shadows lay long and blue to the west and the dew was still on the grass, and I walked in the pleasant spaces of my garden. It was so still...so still...that birds afar off could be heard singing, and once through the crystal air came the voice of a neighbour calling his cows. But the sounds and the silences, the fair sights of meadow and hill I soon put aside, for the lilacs were in bloom and the bush-honeysuckles and the strawberries. Though no movement of the air was perceptible, the lilacs well knew the way of the wind, for if I stood to the north of them the odour was less rich and free than to the south, and I thought I might pose as a prophet of wind and weather upon the basis of this easy magic, and predict that the breezes of the day would be from the north--as, indeed, they later appeared to be.

I went from clump to clump of the lilacs testing and comparing them with great joy and satisfaction. They vary noticeably in odour; the white varieties being the most delicate, while those tending to deep purple are the richest. Some of the newer double varieties seem less fragrant--and I have tested them now many times--than the old-fashioned single varieties which are nearer the native stock. Here I fancy our smooth Jacob has been at work, and in the lucrative process of selection for the eye alone the cunning horticulturist has cheated us of our rightful heritage of fragrance. I have a mind some time to practise the art of burbankry or other kind of wizardy upon the old lilac stock and select for odour alone, securing ravishing original varieties--indeed, whole new gamuts of fragrance.

I should devise the most animating names for my creations, such as the Double Delicious, the Air of Arcady, the Sweet Zephyr, and others even more inviting, which I should enjoy inventing. Though I think surely I could make my fortune out of this interesting idea, I present it freely to a scent-hungry world--here it is, gratis!--for I have my time so fully occupied during all of this and my next two or three lives that I cannot attend to it.

I have felt the same defect in the cultivated roses. While the odours are rich, often of cloying sweetness, or even, as in certain white roses, having a languor as of death, they never for me equal the fragrance of the wild sweet rose that grows all about these hills, in old tangled fence rows, in the lee of meadow boulders, or by some unfrequented roadside. No other odour I know awakens quite such a feeling--light like a cloud, suggesting free hills, open country, sunny air; and none surely has, for me, such an after-call. A whiff of the wild rose will bring back in all the poignancy of sad happiness a train of ancient memories old faces, old scenes, old loves--and the wild thoughts I had when a boy. The first week of the wild-rose blooming, beginning here about the twenty-fifth of June, is always to me a memorable time.

I was a long time learning how to take hold of nature, and think now with some sadness of all the life I lost in former years. The impression the earth gave me was confused: I was as one only half awake. A fine morning made me dumbly glad, a cool evening, after the heat of the day, and the work of it, touched my spirit restfully; but I could have explained neither the one nor the other. Gradually as I looked about me I began to ask myself, "Why is it that the sight of these common hills and fields gives me such exquisite delight? And if it is beauty, why is it beautiful? And if I am so richly rewarded by mere glimpses, can I not increase my pleasure with longer looks?"

I tried longer looks both at nature and at the friendly human creatures all about me. I stopped often in the garden where I was working, or loitered a moment in the fields, or sat down by the roadside, and thought intently what it was that so perfectly and wonderfully surrounded me; and thus I came to have some knowledge of the Great Secret. It was, after all, a simple matter, as such matters usually are when we penetrate them, and consisted merely in shutting out all other impressions, feelings, thoughts, and concentrating the full energy of the attention upon what it was that I saw or heard at that instant.

At one moment I would let in all the sounds of the earth, at another all the sights. So we practise the hand at one time, the foot at another, or learn how to sit or to walk, and so acquire new grace for the whole body. Should we do less in acquiring grace for the spirit? It will astonish one who has not tried it how full the world is of sounds commonly unheard, and of sights commonly unseen, but in their nature, like the smallest blossoms, of a curious perfection and beauty.

Out of this practice grew presently, and as it seems to me instinctively, for I cannot now remember the exact time of its beginning, a habit of repeating under my breath, or even aloud, and in a kind of singsong voice, fragmentary words and sentences describing what it was that I saw or felt at the moment, as, for example:

"The pink blossoms of the wild crab-apple trees I see from the hill.... The reedy song of the wood thrush among the thickets of the wild cherry.... The scent of peach leaves, the odour of new-turned soil in the black fields.... The red of the maples in the marsh, the white of apple trees in bloom.... I cannot find Him out--nor know why I am here...."

Some form of expression, however crude, seemed to reenforce and intensify the gatherings of the senses; and these words, afterward remembered, or even written down in the little book I sometimes carried in my pocket, seemed to awaken echoes, however faint, of the exaltation of that moment in the woods or fields, and enabled me to live twice where formerly I had been able to live but once.

It was by this simple process of concentrating upon what I saw or heard that I increased immeasurably my own joy of my garden and fields and the hills and marshes all about. A little later, for I was a slow learner, I began to practise the same method with the sense of smell, and still later with the sense of taste. I said to myself, "I will no longer permit the avid and eager eye to steal away my whole attention. I will learn to enjoy more completely all the varied wonders of the earth."

So I tried deliberately shutting the doorways of both sight and hearing, and centring the industry of my spirit upon the flavours of the earth. I tested each odour narrowly, compared it well with remembered odours, and often turned the impression I had into such poor words as I could command.

What a new and wonderful world opened to me then! My takings of nature increased tenfold, a hundredfold, and I came to a new acquaintance with my own garden, my own hills, and all the roads and fields around about--and even the town took on strange new meanings for me. I cannot explain it rightly, but it was as though I had found a new earth here within the old one, but more spacious and beautiful than any I had known before. I have thought, often and often, that this world we live in so dumbly, so carelessly, would be more glorious than the tinsel heaven of the poets if only we knew how to lay hold upon it, if only we could win that complete command of our own lives which is the end of our being.

At first, as I said, I stopped my work, or loitered as I walked, in order to see, or hear, or smell--and do so still, for I have entered only the antechamber of the treasure-house; but as I learned better the modest technic of these arts I found that the practice of them went well with the common tasks of the garden or farm, especially with those that were more or less monotonous, like cultivating corn, hoeing potatoes, and the like.

The air is just as full of good sights and good odours for the worker as for the idler, and it depends only upon the awareness, the aliveness, of our own spirits whether we toil like dumb animals or bless our labouring hours with the beauty of life. Such enjoyment and a growing command of our surroundings are possible, after a little practice, without taking much of that time we call so valuable and waste so sinfully. "I haven't time," says the farmer, the banker, the professor, with a kind of disdain for the spirit of life, when, as a matter of fact, he has all the time there is, all that anybody has--to wit, *this* moment, this great and golden moment!--but knows not how to employ it. He creeps when he might walk, walks when he might run, runs when he might fly--and lives like a woodchuck in the dark body of himself.

Why, there are men in this valley who scout the idea that farming, carpentry, merchantry, are anything but drudgery, defend all the evils known to humankind with the argument that "a man must live," and laugh at any one who sees beauty or charm in being here, in working with the hands, or, indeed, in just living! While they think of themselves cannily as "practical" men, I think them the most impractical men I know, for in a world full of boundless riches they remain obstinately poor. They are unwilling to invest even a few of their dollars unearned in the real wealth of the earth. For it is only the sense of the spirit of life, whether in nature or in other human beings, that lifts men above the beasts and curiously leads them to God, who is the spirit both of beauty and of friendliness. I say truly, having now reached the point in my life where it seems to me I care only for writing that which is most deeply true for me, that I rarely walk in my garden or upon the hills of an evening without thinking of God. It is in my garden that all things become clearer to me, even that miracle whereby one who has offended may still see God; and this I think a wonderful thing. In my garden I understand dimly why evil is in the world, and in my garden learn how transitory it is.

Just now I have come in from work, and will note freshly one of the best odours I have had to-day. As I was working in the corn, a lazy breeze blew across the meadows from the west, and after loitering a moment among the blackberry bushes sought me out where I was busiest. Do you know the scent of the blackberry? Almost all the year round it is a treasure-house of odours, even when the leaves first come out; but it reaches crescendo in blossom time when, indeed, I like it least, for being too strong. It has a curious fragrance, once well called by a poet "the hot scent of the brier," and aromatically hot it is and sharp like the briers themselves. At times I do not like it at all, for it gives me a kind of faintness, while at other times, as to-day, it fills me with a strange sense of pleasure as though it were the very breath of the spicy earth. It is also a rare friend of the sun, for the hotter and brighter the day, the hotter and sharper the scent of the brier.

Many of the commonest and least noticed of plants, flowers, trees, possess a truly fragrant personality if once we begin to know them. I had an adventure in my own orchard, only this spring, and made a fine new acquaintance in a quarter least of all expected. I had started down the lane through the garden one morning in the most ordinary way, with no thought of any special experience, when I suddenly caught a whiff of pure delight that stopped me short.

"What now can *that* be?" and I thought to myself that nature had played some new prank on me.

I turned into the orchard, following my nose. It was not the peach buds, nor the plums, nor the cherries, nor yet the beautiful new coloured leaves of the grape, nor anything I could see along the grassy margin of the pasture. There were other odours all about, old friends of mine, but this was some shy and pleasing stranger come venturing upon my land.

A moment later I discovered a patch of low green verdure upon the ground, and dismissed it scornfully as one of my ancient enemies. But it is this way with enemies, once we come to know them, they often turn out to have a fragrance that is kindly.

Well, this particular fierce enemy was a patch of chickweed. Chickweed! Invader of the garden, cossack of the orchard! I discovered, however, that it was in full bloom and covered with small, star-like white blossoms.

"Well, now," said I, "are you the guilty rascal?"

So I knelt there and took my delight of it and a rare, delicate good odour it was. For several days afterward I would not dig out the patch, for I said to myself, "What a cheerful claim it makes these early days, when most of the earth is still cold and dead, for a bit of immortality."

The bees knew the secret already, and the hens and the blackbirds! And I thought it no loss, but really a new and valuable pleasure, to divert my path down the lane for several days that I might enjoy more fully this new odour, and make a clear acquaintance with something fine upon the earth I had not known before.

CHAPTER II
OF GOOD AND EVIL ODOURS

Of all times of the day for good odours I think the early morning the very best, although the evening just after sunset, if the air falls still and cool, is often as good. Certain qualities or states of the atmosphere seem to favour the distillation of good odours and I have known times even at midday when the earth was very wonderful to smell. There is a curious, fainting fragrance that comes only with sunshine and still heat. Not long ago I was cutting away a thicket of wild spiraea which was crowding in upon the cultivated land. It was a hot day and the leaves wilted quickly, giving off such a penetrating, fainting fragrance that I let the branches lie where they fell the afternoon through and came often back to smell of them, for it was a fine thing thus to discover an odour wholly new to me.

I like also the first wild, sweet smell of new-cut meadow grass, not the familiar odour of new-mown hay, which comes a little later, and is worthy of its good report, but the brief, despairing odour of grass just cut down, its juices freshly exposed to the sun. One, as it richly in the fields at the mowing. I like also the midday smell of peach leaves and peach-tree bark at the summer priming: and have never let any one else cut out the old canes from the blackberry rows in my garden for the goodness of the scents which wait upon that work.

Another odour I have found animating is the odour of burning wastage in new clearings or in old fields, especially in the evening when the smoke drifts low along the land and takes to itself by some strange chemical process the tang of earthy things. It is a true saying that nothing will so bring back the emotion of a past time as a remembered odour. I have had from a whiff of fragrance caught in a city street such a vivid return of an old time and an old, sad scene that I have stopped, trembling there, with an emotion long spent and I thought forgotten.

Once in a foreign city, passing a latticed gateway that closed in a narrow court, I caught the odour of wild sweet balsam. I do not know now where it came from, or what could have caused it--but it stopped me short where I stood, and the solid brick walls of that city rolled aside like painted curtains, and the iron streets dissolved before my eyes, and with the curious dizziness of nostalgia, I was myself upon the hill of my youth--with the gleaming river in the valley, and a hawk sailing majestically in the high blue of the sky, and all about and everywhere the balsams--and the balsams--full of the sweet, wild odours of the north, and of dreaming boyhood.

And there while my body, the shell of me, loitered in that strange city, I was myself four thousand miles and a quarter of a century away, reliving, with a conscious passion that boyhood never knew, a moment caught up, like a torch, out of the smouldering wreckage of the past.

Do not tell me that such things die! They all remain with us-all the sights, and sounds, and thoughts of by-gone times awaiting only the whiff from some latticed gateway, some closed-in court to spring again into exuberant life. If only we are ready for the great moment!

As for the odour of the burning wastage of the fields at evening I scarcely know if I dare say it. I find it produces in the blood of me a kind of primitive emotion, as though it stirred memories older than my present life. Some drowsy cells of the brain awaken to a familiar stimulus--the odour of the lodge-fire of the savage, the wigwam of the Indian. Racial memories!

But it is not the time of the day, nor the turn of the season, nor yet the way of the wind that matters most but the ardour and glow we ourselves bring to the fragrant earth. It is a sad thing to reflect that in a world so overflowing with goodness of smell, of fine sights and sweet sounds, we pass by hastily and take so little of them. Days pass when we see no beautiful sight, hear no sweet sound, smell no memorable odour: when we exchange no single word of deeper understanding with a friend. We have lived a day and added nothing to our lives! A blind, grubbing, senseless life--that!

It is a strange thing, also, that instead of sharpening the tools by which we take hold of life we make studied efforts to dull them. We seem to fear life and early begin to stop our ears and close our eyes lest we hear and see too much: we clog our senses and cloud our minds. We seek dull security and ease and cease longer to desire adventure and struggle. And then--the tragedy of it--the poet we all have in us in youth begins to die, the philosopher in us dies, the martyr in us dies, so that the long, long time beyond youth with so many of us becomes a busy death. And this I think truer of men than of women: beyond forty many women just begin to awaken to power and beauty, but most men beyond that age go on dying. The task of the artist, whether poet, or musician, or painter, is to keep alive the perishing spirit of free adventure in men: to nourish the poet, the prophet, the martyr, we all have in us.

One's sense of smell, like the sense of taste, is sharpest when he is hungry, and I am convinced also that one sees and hears best when unclogged with food, undulled with drink, undrugged with smoke. For me, also, weariness, though not exhaustion, seems to sharpen all the senses. Keenness goes with leanness. When I have been working hard or tramping the country roads in the open air and come in weary and hungry at night and catch the fragrance of the evening along the road or upon the hill, or at barn-doors smell the unmilked cows, or at the doorway, the comfortable odours of cooking supper how good that all is! At such times I know Esau to the core: the forthright, nature-loving, simple man he was, coming in dabbled with the blood of hunted animals and hungry for the steaming pottage.

It follows that if we take excessive joys of one sense, as of taste, nature, ever seeking just balances, deprives us of the full enjoyment of the others, "I am stuffed, cousin," cries Beatrice in the play, "I cannot smell." "I have drunk," remarks the Clown in Arcady, "what are roses to me?" We forget that there are five chords in the great scale of life--sight, hearing, smell, taste, touch and--few of us ever master the chords well enough to get the full symphony of life, but are something like little pig-tailed girls playing Peter Piper with one finger while all the music of the universe is in the Great Instrument, and all to be had for the taking.

Of most evil odours, it can be said that they are temporary or unnecessary: and any unpleasant odour, such as that of fruit sprays in spring, or fertilizer newly spread on the land, can be borne and even welcomed if it is appropriate to the time and place. Some smells, evil at first, become through usage not unpleasant. I once stopped with a wolf-trapper in the north country, who set his bottle of bait outside when I came in. He said it was "good and strong" and sniffed it with appreciation. I agreed with him that it was strong. To him it was not unpleasant, though made of the rancid fat of the muscallonge. All nature seems to strive against evil odours, for when she warns us of decay she is speeding decay: and a manured field produces later the best of all odours. Almost all shut-in places sooner or later acquire an evil odour: and it seems a requisite for good smells that there be plenty of sunshine and air; and so it is with the hearts and souls of men. If they are long shut in upon themselves they grow rancid.

CHAPTER III
FOLLOW YOUR NOSE!

"Listen to the Exhortation of the Dawn--
Look to this day! For it is Life,
The very Life of Life!"

On a spring morning one has only to step out into the open country, lift his head to the sky--and follow his nose....

It was a big and golden morning, and Sunday to boot, and I walked down the lane to the lower edge of the field, where the wood and the marsh begin. The sun was just coming up over the hills and all the air was fresh and clear and cool. High in the heavens a few fleecy clouds were drifting, and the air was just enough astir to waken the hemlocks into faint and sleepy exchanges of confidence.

It seemed to me that morning that the world was never before so high, so airy, so golden, All filled to the brim with the essence of sunshine and spring morning-- so that one's spirit dissolved in it, became a part of it. Such a morning! Such a morning!

From that place and just as I was I set off across the open land.

It was the time of all times for good odours--soon after sunrise--before the heat of the day had drawn off the rich distillations of the night.

In that keen moment I caught, drifting, a faint but wild fragrance upon the air, and veered northward full into the way of the wind. I could not at first tell what this particular odour was, nor separate it from the general good odour of the earth; but I followed it intently across the moor-like open land. Once I thought I had lost it entirely, or that the faint northern airs had shifted, but I soon caught it clearly again, and just as I was saying to myself, "I've got it, I've got it!"--for it is a great pleasure to identify a friendly odour in the fields--I saw, near the bank of the brook, among ferns and raspberry bushes, a thorn-apple tree in full bloom.

"So there you are!" I said.

I hastened toward it, now in the full current and glory of its fragrance. The sun, looking over the taller trees to the east, had crowned the top of it with gold, so that it was beautiful to see; and it was full of honey bees as excited as I.

A score of feet onward toward the wind, beyond the thorn-apple tree, I passed wholly out of the range of its fragrance into another world, and began trying for some new odour. After one or two false scents, for this pursuit has all the hazards known to the hunter, I caught an odour long known to me, not strong, nor yet very wonderful, but distinctive. It led me still a little distance northward to a sunny slope just beyond a bit of marsh, and, sure enough, I found an old friend, the wild sweet geranium, a world of it, in full bloom, and I sat down there for some time to enjoy it fully.

Beyond that, and across a field wild with tangles of huckleberry bushes and sheep laurel where the bluets and buttercups were blooming, and in shady spots the shy white violet, I searched for the odour of a certain clump of pine trees I discovered long ago. I knew that I must come upon it soon, but could not tell just when or where. I held up a moistened finger to make sure of the exact direction of the wind, and bearing, then, a little eastward, soon came full upon it--as a hunter might surprise a deer in the forest. I crossed the brook a second time and through a little marsh, making it the rule of the game never to lose for an instant the scent I was following--even though I stopped in a low spot to admire a mass of thrifty blue flags, now beginning to bloom--and came thus to the pines I was seeking. They are not great trees, nor noble, but gnarled and angular and stunted, for the soil in that place is poor and thin, and the winds in winter keen; but the brown blanket of needles they spread and the shade they offer the traveller are not less hospitable; nor the fragrance they give off less enchanting. The odour of the pine is one I love.

I sat down there in a place I chose long ago--a place already as familiar with pleasing memories as a favourite room--so that I wonder that some of the notes I have written there do not of themselves exhale the very odour of the pines.

And all about was hung a fair tapestry of green, and the earthy floor was cleanly carpeted with brown, and the roof above was in arched mosaic, the deep, deep blue of the sky seen through the gnarled and knotted branches of the pines. Through a little opening among the trees, as through a window, I could see the cattle feeding in the wide meadows, all headed alike, and yellow butterflies drifted across the open spaces, and there were bumblebees and dragonflies. And presently I heard some one tapping, tapping, at the door of the wood and glancing up quickly I saw my early visitor. There he was, as neighbourly as you please, and not in the least awed by my intrusion; there he was, far out on the limb of a dead tree, stepping energetically up and down, like a sailor reefing a sail, and rapping and tapping as he worked--a downy woodpecker.

"Good morning, sir," I said.

He stopped for scarcely a second, cocked one eye at me, and went back to his work again. Who was I that I should interrupt his breakfast?

And I was glad I was there, and I began enumerating, as though I were the accredited reporter for the **Woodland Gazette**, all the good news of the day.

"The beech trees." said aloud, "have come at last to full leafage. The wild blackberries are ready to bloom, the swamp roses are budded. Brown planted fields I see, and drooping elms, and the young crows cry from their nests on the knoll.... I know now that, whoever I am, whatever I do, I am welcome here; the meadows are as green this spring for Tom the drunkard, and for Jim the thief, as for Jonathan the parson, or for Walt the poet: the wild cherry blooms as richly, and the odour of the pine is as sweet--"

At that moment, like a flame for clearness, I understood some of the deep and simple things of life, as that we are to be like the friendly pines, and the elm trees, and the open fields, and reject no man and judge no man. Once, a long time ago, I read a sober treatise by one who tried to prove with elaborate knowledge that, upon the whole, good was triumphant in this world, and that probably there was a God, and I remember going out dully afterward upon the hill, for I was weighed down with a strange depression, and the world seemed to me a hard, cold, narrow place where good must be heavily demonstrated in books. And as I sat there the evening fell, a star or two came out in the clear blue of the sky, and suddenly it became all simple to me, so that I laughed aloud at that laborious big-wig for spending so many futile years in seeking doubtful proof of what he might have learned in one rare home upon my hill. And far more than he could prove far more.

As I came away from that place I knew I should never again be quite the same person I was before.

Well, we cannot remain steadily upon the heights. At least I cannot, and would not if I could. After I have been out about so long on such an adventure as this, something lets go inside of me, and I come down out of the mountain--and yet know deeply that I have been where the bush was burning; and have heard the Voice in the Fire.

So it was yesterday morning. I realized suddenly that I was hungry--commonly, coarsely hungry. My whole attention, I was going to say my whole soul, shifted to the thought of ham and eggs! This may seem a tremendous anti-climax, but it is, nevertheless, a sober report of what happened. At the first onset of this new mood, the ham-and-eggs mood, let us call it, I was a little ashamed or abashed at the remembrance of my wild flights, and had a laugh at the thought of myself floundering around in the marshes and fields a mile from home, when Harriet, no doubt, had breakfast waiting for me! What absurd, contradictory, inconsistent, cowardly creatures we are, anyway!

The house seemed an inconceivable distance away, and the only real thing in the world the gnawing emptiness under my belt. And I was wet to my knees, and the tangled huckleberry bashes and sheep laurel and hardback I had passed through so joyously a short time before now clung heavily about my legs as I struggled through them. And the sun was hot and high--and there were innumerable small, black buzzing flies.

To cap the climax, whom should I meet as I was crossing the fence into the lower land but my friend Horace, He had been out early looking for a cow that had dropped her calf in the woods, and was now driving them slowly up the lane, the cow a true pattern of solicitous motherhood, the calf a true pattern of youth, dashing about upon uncertain legs.

"Takin' the air, David?"

I amuse Horace. Horace is an important man in this community. He has big, solid barns, and money in the bank, and a reputation for hardheadedness. He is also known as a "driver"; and has had sore trouble with a favourite son. He believes in "goin' it slow" and "playin' safe," and he is convinced that "ye can't change human nature."

His question came to me with a kind of shock. I imagined with a vividness impossible to describe what Horace would think if I answered him squarely and honestly, if I were to say:

"I've been down in the marshes following my nose--enjoying the thorn apples and the wild geraniums, talking with a woodpecker and reporting the morning news of the woods for an imaginary newspaper."

I was hungry, and in a mood to smile at myself anyway (good-humouredly and forgivingly as we always smile at ourselves!) before I met Horace, and the flashing vision I had of Horace's dry, superior smile finished me. Was there really anything in this world but cows and calves, and great solid barns, and oatcrops, and cash in the bank?

"Been in the brook?" asked Horace, observing my wet legs.

Talk about the courage to face cannon and Cossacks! It is nothing to the courage required to speak aloud in broad daylight of the finest things we have in us! I was not equal to it.

"Oh, I've been down for a tramp in the marsh," I said, trying to put him off.

But Horace is a Yankee of the Yankees and loves nothing better than to chase his friends into corners with questions, and leave them ultimately with the impression that they are somehow less sound, sensible, practical, than he is and he usually proves it, not because he is right, but because he is sure, and in a world of shadowy half-beliefs and half-believers he is without doubts.

"What ye find down there?" asked Horace.

"Oh, I was just looking around to see how the spring was coming on."

"Hm-m," said Horace, eloquently, and when I did not reply, he continued, "Often git out in the morning as early as this?"

"Yes," I said, "often."

"And do you find things any different now from what they would be later in the day?"

At this the humour of the whole situation dawned on me and I began to revive. When things grow hopelessly complicated, and we can't laugh, we do either one of two things: we lie or we die. But if we can laugh, we can fight! And be honest!

"Horace," I said, "I know what you are thinking about."

Horace's face remained perfectly impassive, but there was a glint of curiosity in his eye.

"You've been thinking I've been wasting my time beating around down there in the swamp just to look at things and smell of things--which you wouldn't do. You think I'm a kind of impractical dreamer, now, don't you, Horace? I'll warrant you've told your wife just that more than once. Come, now!"

I think I made a rather shrewd hit, for Horace looked uncomfortable and a little foolish.

"Come now, honest!" I laughed and looked him in the eye.

"Waal, now, ye see--"

"Of course you do, and I don't mind it in the least."

A little dry gleam of humour came in his eye.

"Ain't ye?"

It's a fine thing to have it straight out with a friend.

"No," I said, "I'm the practical man and you're the dreamer. I've rarely known in all my life, Horace, such a confirmed dreamer as you are, nor a more impractical one."

Horace laughed.

"How do ye make that out?"

With this my spirit returned to me and I countered with a question as good as his. It is as valuable in argument as in war to secure the offensive.

"Horace, what are you working for, anyhow?"

This is always a devastating shot. Ninety-nine out of every hundred human beings are desperately at work grubbing, sweating, worrying, thinking, sorrowing, enjoying, without in the least knowing why.

"Why, to make a living--same as you," said Horace.

"Oh, come now, if I were to spread the report in town that a poor neighbour of mine, that's you, Horace, was just making his living, that he himself had told me so, what would you say? Horace, what are you working for? It's something more than a mere living."

"Waal, now, I'll tell ye, if ye want it straight, I'm layin' aside a little something for a rainy day."

"A little something!" this in the exact inflection of irony by which here in the country we express our opinion that a friend has really a good deal more laid aside than anybody knows about. Horace smiled also in the exact manner of one so complimented.

"Horace, what are you going to do with that thirty thousand dollars?"

"Thirty thousand!" Horace looks at me and smiles, and I look at Horace and smile.

"Honest now!"

"Waal, I'll tell ye--a little peace and comfort for me and Josie in our old age, and a little something to make the children remember us when we're gone. Isn't that worth working for?"

He said this with downright seriousness. I did not press him further, but if I had tried I could probably have got the even deeper admission of that faith that lies, like bed rock, in the thought of most men--that honesty and decency here will not be without its reward there, however they may define the "there." Some "prophet's paradise to come!"

"I knew it!" I said. "Horace, you're a dreamer, too. You are dreaming of peace and comfort in your old age, a little quiet house in town where you won't have to labour as hard as you do now, where you won't be worried by crops and weather, and where Mrs. Horace will be able to rest after so many years of care and work and sorrow--a kind of earthly heaven! And you are dreaming of leaving a bit to your children and grandchildren, and dreaming of the gratitude they will express. All dreams, Horace!"

"Oh, waal---"

"The fact is, you are working for a dream, and living on dreams--isn't that true?"

"Waal, now, if you mean it that way----"

"I see I haven't got you beaten yet, Horace!"

He smiled broadly,

"We are all amiable enough with our own dreams. You think that what you are working for--your dream--is somehow sounder and more practical than what I am working for."

Horace started to reply, but had scarcely debouched from his trenches when I opened on him with one of my twenty-fours.

"How do you know that you are ever going to be old?"

It hit.

"And if you do grow old, how do you know that thirty thousand dollars--oh, we'll call it that--is really enough, provided you don't lose it before, to buy peace and comfort for you, or that what you leave your children will make either you or them any happier? Peace and comfort and happiness are terribly expensive, Horace--and prices have been going up fast since this war began!"

Horace looked at me uncomfortably, as men do in the world when you shake the foundations of the tabernacle. I have thought since that I probably pressed him too far; but these things go deep with me.

"No, Horace," I said, "you are the dreamer--and the impractical dreamer at that!"

For a moment Horace answered nothing; and we both stood still there in the soft morning sunshine with the peaceful fields and woods all about us, two human atoms struggling hotly with questions too large for us. The cow and the new calf were long out of sight. Horace made a motion as if to follow them up the lane, but I held him with my glittering eye--as I think of it since, not without a kind of amusement at my own seriousness.

"I'm the practical man, Horace, for I want my peace now, and my happiness now, and my God now. I can't wait. My barns may burn or my cattle die, or the solid bank where I keep my deferred joy may fail, or I myself by to-morrow be no longer here."

So powerfully and vividly did this thought take possession of me that I cannot now remember to have said a decent good-bye to Horace (never mind, he knows me!). At least when I was halfway up the hill I found myself gesticulating with one clenched fist and saying to myself with a kind of passion: "Why wait to be peaceful? Why not he peaceful now? Why not be happy now? Why not be rich now?"

For I think it truth that a life uncommanded now is uncommanded; a life unenjoyed now is unenjoyed; a life not lived wisely now is not lived wisely: for the past is gone and no one knows the future.

As for Horace is he convinced that he is an impractical dreamer. Not a bit of it! He was merely flurried for a moment in his mind, and probably thinks me now, more than ever before, just what I think him. Absurd place, isn't it, this world?

So I reached home at last. You have no idea, unless you have tried it yourself, how good breakfast tastes alter a three-mile tramp in the sharp morning air. The odour of ham and eggs, and new muffins, and coffee, as you come up the hill, there is an odour for you! And it was good to see Harriet.

"Harriet," I said, "you are a sight for tired eyes."

CHAPTER IV
THE GREEN PEOPLE

I have always had a fondness, when upon my travels about the world of the near-by woods and fields, for nipping a bit of a twig here and there and tasting the tart or bitter quality of it. I suppose the instinct descends to me from the herbivorous side of my distant ancestry. I love a spray of white cedar, especially the spicy, sweet inside bark, or a pine needle, or the tender, sweet, juicy end of a spike of timothy grass drawn slowly from its close-fitting sheath, or a twig of the birch that tastes like wintergreen.

I think this no strange or unusual instinct, for I have seen many other people doing it, especially farmers around here, who go through the fields nipping the new oats, testing the red-top, or chewing a bit of sassafras bark. I have in mind a clump of shrubbery in the town road, where an old house once stood, of the kind called here by some the "sweet-scented shrub," and the brandies of it nearest the road are quite clipped and stunted I'm being nipped at by old ladies who pass that way and take to it like cat to catnip.

For a long time this was a wholly unorganized, indeed all but unconscious, pleasure, a true pattern of the childish way we take hold of the earth; but when I began to come newly alive to all things as I have already related--I chanced upon this curious, undeveloped instinct.

"What is it I have here?" I asked myself, for I thought this might be a new handle for getting hold of nature.

Along one edge of my field is a natural hedge of wild cherry, young elms and ashes, dogwood, black raspberry bushes and the like, which has long been a plea-sure to the eye, especially in the early morning when the shadows of it lie long and cool upon the meadow. Many times I have walked that way to admire it, or to listen for the catbirds that nest there, or to steal upon a certain gray squirrel who comes out from his home in the chestnut tree on a fine morning to inspect his premises.

It occurred to me one day that I would make the acquaintance of this hedge in a new way; so I passed slowly along it where the branches of the trees brushed my shoulder and picked a twig here and there and bit it through. "This is cherry," I said; "this is elm, this is dogwood." And it was a fine adventure to know old friends in new ways, for I had never thought before to test the trees and shrubs by their taste and smell. After that, whenever I passed that way, I closed my eyes and tried for further identifications by taste, and was soon able to tell quickly half a dozen other varieties of trees, shrubs, and smaller plants along that bit of meadow.

Presently, as one who learns to navigate still water near shore longs for more thrilling voyages, I tried the grassy old roads in the woods, where young trees and other growths were to be found in great variety: and had a joy of it I cannot describe, for old and familiar places were thus made new and wonderful to me. And when I think of those places, now, say in winter, I grasp them more vividly and strongly than ever I did before, for I think not only how they look, but how they taste and smell, and I even know many of the growing things by the touch of them. It is certain that our grasp of life is in direct proportion to the variety and warmth of the ways in which we lay hold of it. No thought no beauty and no joy.

On these excursions I have often reflected that if I were blind, I should still find here unexplored joys of life, and should make it a point to know all the friendly trees and shrubs around about by the taste or smell or touch of them. I think seriously that this method of widening the world of the blind, and increasing their narrower joys, might well be developed, though it would be wise for such as do take it to borrow first the eyes of a friend to see that no poison ivy, which certain rascally birds plant along our fences and hedges, is lurking about.

Save for this precaution I know of nothing that will injure the taster, though he must be prepared, here and there, for shocks and thrills of bitterness. A lilac leaf, for example, and to a scarcely lesser degree the willow and the poplar are, when bitten through, of a penetrating and intense bitterness; but do no harm, and will daunt no one who is really adventurous. There is yet to be written a botany, or, better yet, a book of nature, for the blind.

It is by knowing human beings that we come to understand them, and by understanding them come to love them, and so it is with the green people. When I was a boy in the wild north country trees were enemies to be ruthlessly fought--to be cut down, sawed, split, burned--anything to be rid of them. The ideal in making a home place was to push the forest as far away from it as possible. But now, when I go to the woods, it is like going among old and treasured friends, and with riper acquaintance the trees come to take on, curiously, a kind of personality, so that I am much fonder of some trees than of others, and instinctively seek out the companionship of certain trees in certain moods, as one will his friends.

I love the unfolding beeches in spring, and the pines in winter; the elms I care for afar off, like great aloof men, whom I can admire; but for friendly confidences give me an apple tree in an old green meadow.

In this more complete understanding I have been much aided by getting hold of my friends of the hedges and hills in the new ways I have described. At times I even feel that I have become a fully accepted member of the Fraternity of the Living Earth, for I have already received many of the benefits which go with that association; and I know now for a certainty that it makes no objection to its members because they are old, or sad, or have sinned, but welcomes them all alike.

The essential taste of the cherry and peach and all their numerous relatives is, in variation, that of the peach pit, so that the whole tribe may be easily recognized, though it was some time before I could tell with certainty the peach from the cherry. The oak shoot, when chewed a little, tastes exactly like the smell of new oak lumber; the maple has a peculiar taste and smell of its own that I can find no comparison for, and the poplar is one of the bitterest trees that ever I have tasted. The trees--pines, spruces, hemlocks, balsams, cedars--are to me about the pleasantest of all, both in taste and odour, and though the spruces and pines taste and smell much alike at first, one soon learns to distinguish them. The elm has a rather agreeable, nondescript, bitterish taste, but the linden is gummy and of a mediocre quality, like the tree itself, which I dislike. Some of the sweetest flowering shrubs, such as the lilac, have the bitterest of leaves and twigs or, like certain kinds of clematis, have a seed that when green is sharper than cayenne pepper, while others, like the rose, are pleasanter in flavour. The ash tree is not too bitter and a little sour.

I give here only a few of the commoner examples, for I wish to make this no tedious catalogue of the flavours of the green people. I am not a scientist, nor would wish to be taken for one. Only last winter I had my pretensions sadly shocked when I tasted twigs cut from various trees and shrubs and tried to identify them by taste or by smell, and while it was a pleasing experiment I found I could not certainly place above half of them; partly, no doubt, because many growing things keep their flavours well wrapped up in winter. No, I have not gone far upon this pleasant road, but neither am I in any great hurry; for there yet remains much time in this and my future lives to conquer the secrets of the earth. I plan to devote at least one entire life to science, and may find I need several!

One great reason why the sense of taste and the sense of smell have not the same honour as the sense of sight or of hearing is that no way has yet been found to make a true art of either. For sight, we have painting, sculpturing, photography, architecture, and the like; and for hearing, music; and for both, poetry and the drama. But the other senses are more purely personal, and have not only been little studied or thought about, but are the ones least developed, and most dimmed and clogged by the customs of our lives.

For the sense of smell we have, indeed, the perfumer's art, but a poor rudimentary art it is, giving little freedom for the artist who would draw his inspirations freshly from nature. I can, indeed, describe poorly in words the odours of this June morning--the mingled lilacs, late wild cherries, new-broken soil, and the fragrance of the sun on green verdure, for there are here both lyrical and symphonic odours--but how inadequate it is! I can tell you what I feel and smell and taste, and give you, perhaps, a desire another spring to spend the months of May and June in the country, but I can scarcely make you live again the very moment of life I have lived, which is the magic quality of the best art. The art of the perfumer which, like all crude art, thrives upon blatancy, does not make us go to gardens, or love the rose, but often instils in us a kind of artificiality, so that perfumes, so far from being an inspiration to us, increasing our lives, become often the badge of the abnormal, used by those unsatisfied with simple, clean, natural things.

And as a people deficient in musical art delights in ragtime tunes, so a people deficient in the true art of tasting and smelling delights in ragtime odours and ragtime tastes.

I do not know that the three so-called lesser senses will ever be organized to the point where they are served by well-established arts, but this I do know--that there are three great ways of entering upon a better understanding of this magic earth which are now neglected.

I think we have come upon hasty and heated days, and are too much mastered by the god of hurry and the swift and greedy eye. We accept flashing pictures of life for life itself; we rush here and rush there and, having arrived, rush away again--to what sensible purpose? Be still a little! Be still!

I do not mean by stillness, stagnation not yet lazy contentment, but life more deeply thought about, more intensely realized, an activity so concentrated that it is quiet. Be still then!

So it is that, though I am no worshipper of the old, I think the older gardeners had in some ways a better practice of the art than we have, for they planted not for the eye alone but for the nose and the sense of taste and even, in growing such plants as the lamb's tongue, to gratify, curiously, the sense of touch. They loved the scented herbs, and appropriately called them simples. Some of these old simples I am greatly fond of, and like to snip a leaf as I go by to smell or taste; but many of them, I here confess, have for me a rank and culinary odour--as sage and thyme and the bold scarlet monarda, sometimes called bergamot.

But if their actual fragrance is not always pleasing, and their uses are now grown obscure, I love well the names of many of them--whether from ancient association or because the words themselves fall pleasantly upon the ear, as, for example, sweet marjoram and dill, anise and summer savoury, lavender and sweet basil. Coriander! Caraway! Cumin! And "there's rosemary, that's for remembrance; pray you, love, remember,... there's fennel for you, and columbines: there's rue for you: and here's some for me--" All sweet names that one loves to roll under his tongue.

I have not any great number of these herbs in my own garden, but, when I go among those I do have, I like to call them by their familiar names as I would a digni-fied doctor or professor, if ever I knew him well enough.

It is in this want of balance and quietude that the age fails most. We are all for action, not at all for reflection; we think there are easy ways to knowledge and shortcuts to perfection; we are for laws rather than for life.

And this reminds me inevitably of a mellow-spirited old friend who lives not a thousand miles from here--I must not tell his name--whose greatest word is "proportion." At this moment, as I write, I can hear the roll of his resonant old voice on the syllable p-o-r--prop-o-rtion. He is the kind of man good to know and to trust.

If ever I bring him a hard problem, as, indeed, I delight to do, it is a fine thing to see him square himself to meet it. A light comes in his eye, he draws back his chin a little and exclaims occasionally: "Well--well!"

He will have all the facts and circumstances fully mobilized, standing up side by side before him like an awkward squad, and there's nothing more awkward than some facts that have to stand out squarely in daylight! And he inquires into their ancestry, makes them run out their tongues, and pokes them once or twice in the ribs, to make sure that they are lively and robust facts capable of making a good fight for their lives. He never likes to see any one thing too large, as a church, a party, a reform, a new book, or a new fashion, lest he see something else too small; but will have everything, as he says, in true proportion. If he occasionally favours a little that which is old, solid, well-placed, it is scarcely to be measured to him as a fault in an age so overwhelmed with the shiny new.

He is a fine, up-standing, hearty old gentleman with white hair and rosy cheeks, and the bright eyes of one who has lived all his life with temperance. One incident I cannot resist telling, though it has nothing directly to do with this story, but it will let you know what kind of a man my old friend is, and when all is said, it would be a fine thing to know about any man. Not long ago he was afflicted with a serious loss, a loss that would have crushed some men, but when I met him not long afterward, though the lines around his eyes were grown deeper, he greeted me in his old serene, courtly manner, When I would have comforted him with my sympathy, for I felt myself near enough to speak of his loss, he replied calmly:

"How can we know whether a thing is evil until we reach the end of it? It may be good!"

One of the events I esteem among the finest of the whole year is my old friend's birthday party. Every winter, on the twenty-sixth of February, a party of his friends drop in to see him. Some of us go out of habit, drawn by our affection for the old gentleman; others, I think, he invites, for he knows to perfection the delicate shadings of companionship which divide those who come unbidden from those, not less loved but shyer, who must be summoned.

Now this birthday gathering has one historic ceremony which none of us would miss, because it expresses so completely the essence of our friend's generous and tolerant, but just, nature. He is, as I have said, a temperate man, and dislikes as much as any one I know the whole alcohol business; but living in a community where the struggle for temperance has often been waged intemperately, and where there is a lurking belief that cudgelling laws can make men virtuous, he publishes abroad once a year his declaration of independence.

After we have been with our friend for an hour or so, and are well warmed and happy with the occasion, he rises solemnly and goes to the toby-closet at the end of his generous fireplace, where the apple-log specially cut for the occasion is burning merrily, and as we all fall silent, knowing well what is coming, he unlocks the door and takes from the shelf a bottle of old peach brandy which, having uncorked, he gravely smells of and possibly lets his nearest neighbour smell of too. Then he brings from the sideboard a server set with diminutive glasses that have been polished until they shine for the great occasion, and, having filled them all with the ripe liquor, he passes them around to each of us. We have all risen and are becomingly solemn as he now proposes the toast of the year--and it is always the same toast:

"Here's to moderation--in all things!"

He takes a sip or two, and continues:

"Here's to temperance--the queen of the virtues."

So we all drink off our glasses. Our mellow old friend smacks his lips, corks the tall bottle, and returns it to his toby-closet, where it reposes undisturbed for another year.

"And now, gentlemen," he says, heartily, "let us go in to dinner.".…

As I think of it, now that it is written, this story bears no very close relationship to my original subject, and yet it seemed to follow naturally enough as I set it down, and to belong with the simple and well-flavoured things of the garden and fields; and recalling the advice of Cobbett to his nephew on the art of writing, "never to alter a thought, for that which has come of itself into your mind is likely to pass into that of another more readily and with more effect than anything which you can by reflection invent," I leave it here just as I wrote it, hoping that the kinship of my genial old friend with simple and natural and temperate things may plainly appear.

CHAPTER V
PLACES OF RETIREMENT

"Good God, how sweet are all things here!
How beautiful the fields appear!
  How cleanly do we feed and lie!
Lord, what good hours do we keep!
How quietly we sleep!"

CHARLES COTTON (a friend of Izaak Walton)

April 29th.

I have been spending a Sunday of retirement in the woods. I came out with a strange, deep sense of depression, and though I knew it was myself and not the world that was sad, yet I could not put it away from me. ... As I write, the wood seems full of voices, the little rustling of leaves, the minute sounds of twigs chafing together, the cry of frogs from the swamp so steady and monotonous that it scarcely arrests attention. Of odours, a-plenty! Just behind me, so that by turning my head I can see into their cool green depths, are a number of hemlock trees, the breath of which is incalculably sweet. All the earth the very earth itself has a good rich growing odour, pleasant to smell.

These things have been here a thousand years a million years and yet they are not stale, but are ever fresh, ever serene, ever here to loosen one's crabbed spirit and make one quietly happy. It seems to me I could not live if it were not possible often to come thus alone to the woods.

...On later walking I discover that here and there on warm southern slopes the dog-tooth violet is really in bloom, and worlds of hepatica, both lavender and white, among the brown leaves. One of the notable sights of the hillsides at this time of the year is the striped maple, the long wands rising straight and chaste among thickets of less-striking young birches and chestnuts, and having a bud of a delicate pink--a marvel of minute beauty. A little trailing arbutus I found and renewed my joy with one of the most exquisite odours of all the spring; Solomon's seal thrusting up vivid green cornucopias from the lifeless earth, and often near a root or stone the red partridge berries among their bright leaves. The laurel on the hills is sharply visible, especially when among deciduous trees, and along the old brown roads are patches of fresh wintergreen. In a cleft of the hills near the top of Norwottuck, though the day is warm, I found a huge snowbank--the last held trench of old winter, the last guerilla of the cold, driven to the fastnesses of the hills.... I have enjoyed this day without trying. After the first hour or so of it all the worries dropped away, all the ambitions, all the twisted thoughts--

It is strange how much thrilling joy there is in the discovery of the ages-old miracle of returning life in the woods: each green adventurer, each fragrant joy, each bird-call--and the feel of the soft, warm sunshine upon one's back after months of winter. On any terms life is good. The only woe, the only Great Woe, is the woe of never having been born. Sorrow, yes; failure, yes; weakness, yes the sad loss of dear friends--yes! But oh, the good God: I still live!

Being alone without feeling alone is one of the great experiences of life, and he who practises it has acquired an infinitely valuable possession. People fly to crowds for happinesss not knowing that all the happiness they find there they must take with them. Thus they divert and distract that within them which creates power and joy, until by flying always away from themselves, seeking satisfaction from without rather than from within, they become infinitely boresome to themselves, so that they can scarcely bear a moment of their own society.

But if once a man have a taste of true and happy retirement, though it be but a short hour, or day, now and then, he has found, or is beginning to find, a sure place of refuge, of blessed renewal, toward which in the busiest hours he will find his thoughts wistfully stealing. How stoutly will he meet the buffets of the world if he knows he has such a place of retirement where all is well-ordered and full of beauty, and right counsels prevail, and true things are noted.

As a man grows older, if he cultivate the art of retirement, not indeed as an end in itself, but as a means of developing a richer and freer life, he will find his reward growing surer and greater until in time none of the storms or shocks of life any longer disturbs him. He might in time even reach the height attained by Diogenes, of whom Epictetus said, "It was not possible for any man to approach him, nor had any man the means of laying hold upon him to enslave him. He had everything easily loosed, everything only hanging to him. If you laid hold of his property, he would rather have let it go and be yours than he would have followed you for it; if you laid hold of his leg he would have let go his leg: if all of his body, all his poor body; his intimates, friends, country, just the same. For he knew from whence he had them, and from whom and on what conditions."

The best partners of solitude are books. I like to take a book with me in my pocket, although I find the world so full of interesting things--sights, sounds, odours--that often I never read a word in it. It is like having a valued friend with you, though you walk for miles without saying a word to him or he to you: but if you really know your friend, it is a curious thing how, subconsciously, you are aware of what he is thinking and feeling about this hillside or that distant view. And so it is with books. It is enough to have this writer in your pocket, for the very thought of him and what he would say to these old fields and pleasant trees is ever freshly delightful. And he never interrupts at inconvenient moments, nor intrudes his thoughts upon yours unless you desire it.

I do not want long books and least of all story books in the woods--these are for the library--but rather scraps and extracts and condensations from which thoughts can be plucked like flowers and carried for a while in the buttonhole. So it is that I am fond of all kinds of anthologies. I have one entitled "Traveller's Joy," another, "Songs of Nature," and I have lately found the best one I know called "The Spirit of Man" by Robert Bridges, the English laureate. Other little books that fit well in the pocket on a tramp, because they are truly companionable, are Ben Jonson's "Timber," one of the very best, and William Penn's "Fruits of Solitude." An anthology of Elizabethan verse, given me by a friend, is also a good companion.

It is not a discourse or a narrative we want as we walk abroad, but conversation. Neither do we want people or facts or stories, but a person. So I open one of these little books and read therein the thoughtful remark of a wise companion. This

I may reply to, or merely enjoy, as I please. I am in no hurry, as I might be with a living companion, for my book friend, being long dead, is not impatient and gives me time to reply, and is not resentful if I make no reply at all. Submitted to such a test as this few writers, old or new, give continued profit or delight. To be considered in the presence of the great and simple things of nature, or worn long in the warm places of the spirit, a writer must have supreme qualities of sense or humour, a great sensitiveness to beauty, or a genuine love of goodness--but above all he must somehow give us the flavour of personality. He must be a true companion of the spirit.

*   *   *   *   *

There is an exercise given to young soldiers which consists in raising the hands slowly above the head, taking in a full breath at the same time, and then letting them down in such a way as to square the shoulders. This leaves the body erect, the head high, the eyes straight ahead, the lungs full of good air. It is the attitude that every man at arms should wish to take, After a day in the woods I feel some such erectness of spirit, a life of the head, and a clearer and calmer vision, for I have raised up my hands to the heavens, and drawn in the odours and sights and sounds of the good earth.

*   *   *   *   *

One of the great joys of such times of retirement perhaps the greatest of the joys is the return, freshened and sweetened, to the common life. How good then appear the things of the garden and farm, the house and shop, that weariness had staled; how good the faces of friends.

CHAPTER VI
+NO TRESPASS+

I live in a country of beautiful hills, and in the last few years, since I have been here with Harriet, I have made familiar and pleasant acquaintance with several of them....

One hill I know is precious to me for a peculiar reason. Upon the side of it, along the town road, are two or three old farms with lilacs like trees about their doorways, and ancient apple orchards with great gnarly branches, and one has an old garden of hollyhocks, larkspurs, zinnias, mignonette, and I know not how many other old-fashioned flowers. Wild grapes there are along the neglected walls, and in a corner of one of them, by a brook, a mass of sweet currant which in blossom time makes all that bit of valley a bower of fragrance, I have gone that way often in spring for the sheer joy of the friendly odours I had across the ancient stone fences.

The largest and stoniest of the farms is owned by an old man named Howieson. A strange, brown-clad, crooked, crabbed old man, I have seen him often creeping across his fields with his horses. An ineffective worker all his life long, he has scarcely made a living from his stony acres. His farm is tipped up behind upon the hill and runs below to the brook, and the buildings are old and worn, and a rocky road goes by to the town. Once, in more prosperous days, before the factories took over the winter work of these hill farms, the busy families finished shoes, and wove cloth, and plaited straw hats--and one I know was famous for wooden bowls craftily hollowed out of maple knots--and the hill people relied upon their stony fields for little more than their food. But in these later days, the farm industries are gone, the houses are no longer overflowing with children, for there is nothing for children to do, and those who remain are old or discouraged. Some homes have entirely disappeared, so that all that remains is a clump of lilacs or a wild tangle of rose bushes about a grass-covered or bush-grown cellar wall. The last thing to disappear is not that which the old farmers most set their hearts upon, their fine houses and barns or their cultivated fields, but the one touch of beauty they left--lilac clump or rose-tangle.

Old Howieson, with that passion for the sense of possession which thrives best when the realities of possession are slipping away, has posted all his fields with warnings against intrusion. You may not enter this old field, nor walk by this brook, nor climb this hill, for all this belongs, in fee simple, to James Howieson!

For a long time I did not meet James Howieson face to face, though I had often seen his signs, and always with a curious sense of the futility of them. I did not need to enter his fields, nor climb his hill, nor walk by his brook, but as the springs passed and the autumns whitened into winter, I came into more and more complete possession of all those fields that he so jealously posted. I looked with strange joy upon his hill, saw April blossom in his orchard, and May colour the wild grape leaves along his walls. June I smelled in the sweet vernal of his hay fields, and from the October of his maples and beeches I gathered rich crops and put up no hostile signs of ownership, paid no taxes, worried over no mortgage, and often marvelled that he should be so poor within his posted domain and I so rich without.

One who loves a hill, or a bit of valley, will experiment long until he finds the best spot to take his joy of it; and this is no more than the farmer himself does when he experiments year after year to find the best acres for his potatoes, his corn, his oats, his hay. Intensive cultivation is as important in these wider fields of the spirit as in any other. If I consider the things that I hear and see and smell, and the thoughts that go with them or grow out of them, as really valuable possessions, contributing to the wealth of life, I cannot see why I should not willingly give to them a tenth or a hundredth part of the energy and thought I give to my potatoes or my blackberries or to the writing I do.

I chose a place in a field just below Old Howieson's farm, where there is a thorn-apple tree to sit or lie under. From the thorn-apple tree, by turning my head in one direction, I can look up at the crown of the hill with its green hood of oaks and maples and chestnuts, and high above it I can see the clouds floating in the deep sky, or, if I turn my head the other way, for I am a kind of monarch there on the hill and command the world to delight me, I can look off across the pleasant valley with its spreading fields and farmsteads set about with trees, and the town slumbering by the riverside. I come often with a little book in one pocket to read from, and a little book in the other to write in, but I rarely use either the one or the other, for there is far too much to see and think about.

From this spot I make excursions round about, and have had many strange and interesting adventures: and now find thoughts of mine, like lichens, upon all the boulders and old walls and oak trees of that hillside. Sometimes I climb to the top of the hill. If I am in a leisurely mood I walk lawfully around Old Howieson's farm by a kind of wood lane that leads to the summit, but often I cross his walls, all regardless of his trespass signs, and go that way to the top.

It was on one of these lawless excursions in Old Howieson's field that I first saw that strange old fellow who is known hereabout as the Herbman. I came upon him so suddenly that I stopped short, curiously startled, as one is startled at finding anything human that seems less than human. He was kneeling there among the low verdure of a shallow valley, and looked like an old gray rock or some prehistoric animal. I stopped to look at him, but he paid no heed, and seemed only to shrink into himself as though, if he kept silent, he might be taken for stock or stone. I addressed him but he made no answer. I went nearer, with a sensation of uncanny wonder; but he did not so much as glance up at me, though he knew I was there. His old brown basket was near him and the cane beside it. He was gathering pennyroyal.

"Another man who is taking an unexpected crop from Old Howieson's acres," I thought to myself.

I watched him for some moments, quite still, as one might watch a turtle or a woodchuck--and left him there.

Since then I have heard something about him, and seen him once or twice. A strange old man, a wanderer upon the face of the fragrant earth. Spring and summer he wears always an old overcoat, and carries a basket with double covers, very much worn and brown with usage. His cane is of hickory with a crooked root for a handle, this also shiny with age. He gathers bitter-bark, tansy; ginseng, calamus, smartweed, and slippery elm, and from along old fences and barnyards, catnip and boneset, I suppose he lives somewhere, a hole in a log, or the limb of a tree, but no one knows where it is, or how he dries or cures his findings. No one knows his name: perhaps he has forgotten it himself. A name is no great matter anyway. He is called simply the Herbman. He drifts into our valley in the spring, is seen here and there on the hills or in the fields, like the crows or the blackbirds, and disappears in the fall with the robins and the maple leaves. Perhaps he is one of those favoured souls to whom life is all spring and summer.

The age has passed him by, and except for certain furtive old women, few care now for his sovereign remedies.

I met him once in the town road, and he stopped humbly without lifting his eyes, and opening his basket let out into the air such a fragrance of ancient simples as I never smelled before. He said nothing at all; but took out dry bundles of catnip, sassafras, slippery elm, to show me. He had also pennyroyal for healing teas, and calamus and bitter-bark for miseries. I selected a choice assortment of his wares to take home to Harriet, but could get him to name no price. He took what I gave without objection and without thanks, and went his way. A true man of the hills.

As I said, I came often to the field below Old Howieson's farm. I think the old man saw me coming and going, for the road winds along the side of the hill within sight of his house, skirts a bit of wood, and with an unexpected turn comes out triumphantly to the top of the ridge beyond.

At the turn of the road I always disappeared, for I crossed the wall into the field below Old Howieson's farm, and mysteriously failed to appear to the watchful eye upon the ridge beyond. What could be more provoking or suspicious! To go in at one end of a well-travelled road and not to come out in the regular and expected way at the other! Or to be suspected of not being deferential toward trespass signs, or observant of closed ways! How disturbing to all those who dwell tremulously within posted enclosures of whatever sort, or those who base their sense of possession upon stumped paper, or take their God from a book. Men have been crucified for less.

Sooner or later those who cross boundaries clash with those who defend boundaries: and those who adventure offend those who seek security; but it was a long time before I came face to face with Old Man Howieson.

This was the way of it: Well back of Howieson's buildings and reaching upward upon the face of the hill stretches a long and narrow field, a kind of barren back pasture with boulders in it, and gnarly hawthorn trees, and a stunted wild apple or so. A stone fence runs down one side of the cleared land and above it rises the hill.

It is like a great trough or ravine which upon still spring evenings gathers in all the varied odours of Old Howieson's farm and orchard and brings them down to me as I sit in the field below. I need no book then, nor sight of the distant town, nor song of birds, for I have a singular and incomparable album of the good odours of the hill. This is one reason why I chose this particular spot in the fields for my own, and it has given me a secret name for the place which I will not here disclose. If ever you should come this way in May, my friend, I might take you there of an evening, but could warrant you no joy of it that you yourself could not take. But you need not come here, or go there, but stop where you are at this moment, and I here assure you that if you look up, and look in, you, also, will see something of the glory of the world.

One evening I had been upon the hill to seek again the pattern and dimensions of my tabernacle, and to receive anew the tables of the Jaw. I had crossed Old Howieson's field so often that I had almost forgotten it was not my own. It was indeed mine by the same inalienable right that it belonged to the crows that flew across it, or to the partridges that nested in its coverts, or the woodchucks that lived in its walls, or the squirrels in its chestnut trees. It was mine by the final test of all possession--that I could use it.

He came out of a thicket of hemlocks like a wraith of the past, a gray and crabbed figure, and confronted me there in the wide field. I suppose he thought he had caught me at last. I was not at all startled or even surprised, for as I look back upon it now I know that I had always been expecting him. Indeed, I felt a lift of the spirit, the kind of jauntiness with which one meets a crucial adventure.

He stood there for a moment quite silent, a grim figure of denial, and I facing him.

"You are on my land, sir," he said.

I answered him instantly and in a way wholly unexpected to myself:

"You are breathing my air, sir."

He looked at me dully, but with a curious glint of fear in his eye, fear and anger, too.

"Did you see the sign down there? This land is posted."

"Yes," I said, "I have seen your signs. But let me ask you: If I were not here would you own this land any more than you do now? Would it yield you any better crops?"

It is never the way of those who live in posted enclosures, of whatever sort, to reason. They assert.

"This land is posted," said the old man doggedly.

"Are you sure you own it?" I asked. "Is it really yours?"

"My father owned this farm before me," he said, "and my grandfather cleared this field and built these walls. I was born in that house and have lived there all my life."

"Well, then, I must be going--and I will not come here again," I said. "I am sorry I walked on your land--"

I started to go down the hill, but stopped, and said, as though it were an after-thought:

"I have made some wonderful discoveries upon your land, and that hill there. You don't seem to know how valuable this field is.... Good-bye."

With that I took two or three steps down the hill--but felt the old man's hand on my arm.

"Say, mister," he asked, "are you one of the electric company men? Is that high-tension line comin' across here?"

"No," I said, "it is something more valuable than that!"

I walked onward a few steps, as though I was quite determined to get out of his field, but he followed close behind me.

"It ain't the new trolley line, is it?"

"No," I said, "it isn't the trolley line."

"What is it, then?"

In that question, eager and shrill, spoke the dry soul of the old man, the lifelong hope that his clinging ownership of those barren acres would bring him from the outside some miraculous profit.

His whole bearing had changed. He had ceased to be truculent or even fearful, but was now shrilly beseeching, A great wave of compassion came over me, I was sorry for him, imprisoned there within the walls of his own making, and expecting wealth from the outside when there was wealth in plenty within and everywhere about him.

But how could I help him? You can give no valuable thing to any man who has not the vision to take it. If I had told him what I found upon his hill or in his fields he would have thought me--well, crazy; or he would have suspected that under cover of such a quest I hid some evil design. As well talk adventure to an old party man, or growth to a set churchman.

So I left him there within his walls. So often when we think we are barring other people out, we are only barring ourselves in. The last I saw of him as I turned into the road was a gray and crabbed figure standing alone, looking after me, and not far off his own sign:

Sometime, I thought, this old farm will be owned by a man who is also capable of possessing it. More than one such place I know already has been taken by those who value the beauty of the hills and the old walls, and the boulder-strewn fields. One I know is really possessed by a man who long ago had a vision of sheep feeding on fields too infertile to produce profitable crops, and many others have been taken by men who saw forests growing where forests ought to grow. For real possession is not a thing of inheritance or of documents, but of the spirit; and passes by vision and imagination. Sometimes, indeed, the trespass signs stand long--so long that we grow impatient--but nature is in no hurry. Nature waits, and presently the trespass signs rot away, one arm falls off, and lo! where the adventurer found only denial before he is now invited to--"pass." The old walls are conquered by the wild cherries and purple ivy and blackberry bushes, and the old Howiesons sleep in calm forgetfulness of their rights upon the hills they thought they possessed, and all that is left is a touch of beauty--lilac clump and wild-rose tangle.

CHAPTER VII
LOOK AT THE WORLD!

"Give me to struggle with weather and wind;
  Give me to stride through the snow;
Give me the feel of the chill on my cheeks,
  And the glow and the glory within!"

March 17th.

The joy of winter: the downright joy of winter! I tramped to-day through miles of open, snow-clad country. I slipped in the ruts of the roads or ploughed through the drifts in the fields with such a sense of adventure as I cannot describe.

Day before yesterday we had a heavy north wind with stinging gusts of snow. Yesterday fell bright and cold with snow lying fine and crumbly like sugar. To the east of the house where I shovelled a path the heaps are nearly as high as my shoulder....

This perfect morning a faint purplish haze is upon all the hills, with bright sunshine and still, cold air through which the chimney smoke rises straight upward. Hungry crows flap across the fields, or with unaccustomed daring settle close in upon the manure heaps around the barns. All the hillsides glisten and sparkle like cloth of gold, each glass knob on the telephone poles is like a resplendent jewel, and the long morning shadows of the trees lie blue upon the snow. Horses' feet crunch upon the road as the early farmers go by with milk for the creamery--the frosty breath of each driver fluttering aside like a white scarf. Through the still air ordinary voices cut sharply and clearly, and a laugh bounds out across the open country

with a kind of superabundance of joy. I see two men beating their arms as they follow their wood sled. They are bantering one another noisily. I see a man shovelling
snow from his barn doors; as each shovelful rises and scatters, the sun catches it for
an instant and it falls, a silvery shower. ... I tramped to-day through miles of it: and
whether in broken roads or spotless fields, had great joy of it. It was good to stride
through opposing drifts and to catch the tingling air upon one's face. The spring is
beautiful indeed, and one is happy at autumn, but of all the year no other mornings
set the blood to racing like these; none gives a greater sense of youth, strength, or of
the general goodness of the earth.

Give me the winter: give me the winter! Not all winter, but just winter enough,
just what nature sends.

...Dry air in the throat so cold at first as to make one cough; and dry, sharp,
tingling air in the nostrils; frost on beard and eyebrows; cheeks red and crusty, so
that to wrinkle them hurts: but all the body within aglow with warmth and health.
Twice the ordinary ozone in the air, so that one wishes to whistle or sing, and if the
fingers grow chill, what are shoulders for but to beat them around!

*   *   *   *   *

It is a strange and yet familiar experience how all things present their opposites.
Do you enjoy the winter? Your neighbour loathes or fears it. Do you enjoy life? To
your friend it is a sorrow and a heaviness. Even to you it is not always alike. Though
the world itself is the same to-day as it was yesterday and will be to-morrow--the
same snowy fields and polar hills, the same wintry stars, the same infinitely alluring
variety of people--yet to-day you, that were a god, have become a grieving child.

Even at moments when we are well pleased with the earth we often have a
wistful feeling that we should conceal it lest it hurt those borne down by circumstances too great or too sad for them. What is there to offer one who cannot respond
gladly to the beauty of the fields, or opens his heart widely to the beckoning of
friends? And we ask ourselves: Have I been tried as this man has? Would I be happy
then? Have I been wrung with sorrow, worn down by ill-health, buffeted with in-
justice as this man has? Would I be happy then?

I saw on my walk to-day an old woman with a crossed shawl upon her breast creeping out painfully to feed her hens. She lives on a small, ill-kept farm I have known for years. She is old and poor and asthmatic, and the cold bites through her with the sharpness of knives. The path to the hen-house is a kind of via dolorosa, a terror of slipperiness and cold. She might avoid it: her son, worthless as he is, might do it for her, but she clings to it as she clings to her life. It is the last reason for staying here! But the white fields and drifted roads are never joyfully met, never desired. She spends half the summer dreading the return of winter from the severities of which she cannot escape.

Nor is it all mere poverty, though she is poor, for there are those who would help to send her away, but she will not go. She is wrapped about with Old Terrors, Ancient Tyrannies--that Terror of the Unknown which is more painful even than the Terror of the Known: those Tyrannies of Habit and of Place which so often and so ruthlessly rule the lives of the old. She clings desperately to the few people she knows ("'tis hard to die among strangers!") and the customs she has followed all her life. Against the stark power of her tragic helplessness neither the good nor the great of the earth may prevail. This reality too....

I had a curious experience not long ago: One of those experiences which light up as in a flash some of the fundamental things of life. I met a man in the town road whom I have come to know rather more than slightly. He is a man of education and has been "well-off" in the country sense, is still, so far as I know, but he has a sardonic outlook upon life. He is discouraged about human nature. Thinks that politics are rotten, and that the prices of potatoes and bread are disgraceful. The state of the nation, and of the world, is quite beyond temperate expression. Few rays of joy seem to illuminate his pathway.

As we approached in the town road I called out to him:

"Good morning."

He paused and, to my surprise, responded:

"Are you happy?"

It had not occurred to me for some time whether I was happy or not, so I replied:

"I don't know; why do you ask?"

He looked at me in a questioning, and I thought rather indignant, way.

"Why shouldn't a man be happy?" I pressed him.

"Why *should* he be? Answer me that!" he responded, "Why should he be? Look at the world!"

With that he passed onward with a kind of crushing dignity.

I have laughed since when I have recalled the tone of his voice as he said, "Look at the world!" Gloomy and black it was. It evidently made him indignant to be here.

But at the moment his bitter query, the essential attitude of spirit which lay behind it, struck into me with a poignancy that stopped me where I stood. Was I, then, all wrong about the world? I actually had a kind of fear lest when I should look up again I should find the earth grown wan and bleak and unfriendly, so that I should no longer desire it.

"Look at the world!" I said aloud.

And with that I suddenly looked all around me and it is a strange, deep thing, as I have thought of it since, how the world came back upon me with a kind of infinite, calm assurance, as beautiful as ever it was. There were the hills and the fields and the great still trees--and the open sky above. And even as I looked down the road and saw my sardonic old friend plodding through the snow--his very back frowning--I had a sense that he belonged in the picture, too--and couldn't help himself. That he even had a kind of grace, and gave a human touch to that wintry scene! He had probably said a great deal more than he meant!

Look at the world!

Well, look at it.

CHAPTER VIII
A GOOD APPLE

I am made immortal by apprehending my possession of incorruptible goods."
I have just had one of the pleasant experiences of life. From time to time, these
brisk winter days, I like to walk across the fields to Horace's farm. I take a new
way each time and make nothing of the snow in the fields or the drifts along
the fences....

"Why," asks Harriet, "do you insist on struggling through the snow when
there's a good beaten road around?"

"Harriet," I said, "why should any one take a beaten road when there are new
and adventurous ways to travel?"

When I cross the fields I never know at what moment I may come upon some
strange or surprising experience, what new sights I may see, what new sounds I
may hear, and I have the further great advantage of appearing unexpectedly at Horace's farm. Sometimes I enter by the cow lane, sometimes by way of the old road
through the wood-lot, or I appear casually, like a gust of wind, around the corner
of the barn, or I let Horace discover me leaning with folded arms upon his cattle
fence. I have come to love doing this, for unexpectedness in visitors, as in religion
and politics, is disturbing to Horace and, as sand-grits in oysters produce pearls, my
unexpected appearances have more than once astonished new thoughts in Horace,
or yielded pearly bits of native humour.

Ever since I have known him, Horace has been rather high-and-mighty with
me; but I know he enjoys my visits, for I give him always, I think, a pleasantly renewed sense of his own superiority. When he sees me his eye lights up with the
comfortable knowledge that he can plough so much better than I can, that his corn
grows taller than mine, and his hens lay more eggs. He is a wonderfully practical

man, is Horace; hard-headed, they call it here. And he never feels so superior, I think, as when he finds me sometimes of a Sunday or an evening walking across the fields where my land joins his, or sitting on a stone fence, or lying on my back in the pasture under a certain friendly thorn-apple tree. This he finds it difficult to understand, and thinks it highly undisciplined, impractical, no doubt reprehensible.

One incident of the sort I shall never forget. It was on a June day only a year or so after I came here, and before Horace knew me as well as he does now. I had climbed the hill to look off across his own high-field pasture, where the white daisies, the purple fleabane, and the buttercups made a wild tangle of beauty among the tall herd's grass. Light airs moved billowing across the field, bobolinks and meadow larks were singing, and all about were the old fences, each with its wild hedgerow of choke cherry, young elms, and black raspberry bushes, and beyond, across miles and miles of sunny green countryside, the mysterious blue of the ever-changing hills. It was a spot I loved then, and have loved more deeply every year since.

Horace found me sitting on the stone fence which there divides our possessions; I think he had been observing me with amusement for some time before I saw him, for when I looked around his face wore a comfortably superior, half-disdainful smile.

"David," said he, "what ye doin' here?"

"Harvesting my crops," I said.

He looked at me sharply to see if I was joking, but I was perfectly sober.

"Harvestin' yer crops?"

"Yes," I said, the fancy growing suddenly upon me, "and just now I've been taking a crop from the field you think you own."

I waved my hand to indicate his high-field pasture.

"Don't I own it?"

"No, Horace, I'm sorry to say, not all of it. To be frank with you, since I came here, I've quietly acquired an undivided interest in that land. I may as well tell you first as last. I'm like you, Horace, I'm reaching out in all directions."

I spoke in as serious a voice as I could command: the tone I use when I sell potatoes. Horace's smile wholly disappeared. A city feller like me was capable of anything!

"How's that?" he exclaimed sharply. "What do you mean? That field came down to me from my grandfather Jamieson."

I continued to look at Horace with great calmness and gravity.

"Judging from what I now know of your title, Horace," said I, "neither your grandfather Jamieson nor your father ever owned all of that field. And I've now acquired that part of it, in fee simple, that neither they nor you ever really had."

At this Horace began to look seriously worried. The idea that any one could get away from him anything that he possessed, especially without his knowledge, was terrible to him.

"What do you mean, Mr. Grayson?"

He had been calling me "David," but he now returned sharply to "Mister." In our country when we "Mister" a friend something serious is about to happen. It's the signal for general mobilization.

I continued to look Horace rather coldly and severely in the eye.

"Yes," said I, "I've acquired a share in that field which I shall not soon surrender."

An unmistakable dogged look came into Horace's face, the look inherited from generations of land-owning, home-defending, fighting ancestors. Horace is New England of New England.

"Yes," I said, "I have already had two or three crops from that field."

"Huh!" said Horace. "I've cut the grass and I've cut the rowen every year since you bin here. What's more, I've got the money fer it in the bank."

He tapped his fingers on the top of the wall.

"Nevertheless, Horace," said I, "I've got my crops, also, from that field, and a steady income, too."

"What crops?"

"Well, Eve just now been gathering in one of them. What do you think of the value of the fleabane, and the daisies, and the yellow five-finger in that field?"

"Huh!" said Horace.

"Well, I've just been cropping them. And have you observed the wind in the grass--and those shadows along the southern wall? Aren't they valuable?"

"Huh!" said Horace.

"I've rarely seen anything more beautiful," I said, "than this field and the view across it--I'm taking that crop now, and later I shall gather in the rowen of goldenrod and aster, and the red and yellow of the maple trees--and store it all away in *my* bank--to live on next winter."

It was some time before either of us spoke again, but I could see from the corner of my eye that mighty things were going on inside of Horace; and suddenly he broke out into a big laugh and clapped his knee with his hand in a way he has.

"Is that all!" said Horace.

I think it only confirmed him in the light esteem in which he held me. Though I showed him unmeasured wealth in his own fields, ungathered crops of new enjoyment, he was unwilling to take them, but was content with hay. It is a strange thing to me, and a sad one, how many of our farmers (and be it said in a whisper, other people, too) own their lands without ever really possessing them: and let the most precious crops of the good earth go to waste.

After that, for a long time, Horace loved to joke me about my crops and his. A joke with Horace is a durable possession.

"S'pose you think that's your field," he'd say.

"The best part of it," I'd return, "but you can have all I've taken, and there'll still be enough for both of us."

"You're a queer one!" he'd say, and then add sometimes, dryly, "but there's one crop ye don't git, David," and he'd tap his pocket where he carries his fat, worn, leather pocket-book. "And as fer feelin's, it can't be beat."

So many people have the curious idea that the only thing the world desires enough to pay its hard money for is that which can be seen or eaten or worn. But there never was a greater mistake. While men will haggle to the penny over the price of hay, or fight for a cent more to the bushel of oats, they will turn out their very pockets for strange, intangible joys, hopes, thoughts, or for a moment of peace in a feverish world the unknown great possessions.

So it was that one day, some months afterward, when we had been thus bantering each other with great good humour, I said to him:

"Horace, how much did you get for your hay this year?"

"Off that one little piece," he replied, "I figger fifty-two dollars."

"Well, Horace," said I, "I have beaten you. I got more out of it this year than you did."

"Oh, I know what you mean----"

"No, Horace, you don't. This time I mean just what you do: money, cash, dollars."

"How's that, now?"

"Well, I wrote a little piece about your field, and the wind in the grass, and the hedges along the fences, and the weeds among the timothy, and the fragrance of it all in June and sold it last week----" I leaned over toward Horace and whispered behind my hand--in just the way he tells me the price he gets for his pigs.

"What!" he exclaimed.

Horace had long known that I was "a kind of literary feller," but his face was now a study in astonishment.

"*What?*"

Horace scratched his head, as he is accustomed to do when puzzled, with one finger just under the rim of his hat.

"Well, I vum!" said he.

Here I have been wandering all around Horace's barn--in the snow--getting at the story I really started to tell, which probably supports Horace's conviction that I am an impractical and unsubstantial person. If I had the true business spirit I should have gone by the beaten road from my house to Horace's, borrowed the singletree I went for, and hurried straight home. Life is so short when one is after dollars! I should not have wallowed through the snow, nor stopped at the top of the hill to look for a moment across the beautiful wintry earth--gray sky and bare wild trees and frosted farmsteads with homely smoke rising from the chimneys--I should merely have brought home a singletree--and missed the glory of life! As I reflect upon it now, I believe it took me no longer to go by the fields than by the road; and I've got the singletree as securely with me as though I had not looked upon the beauty of the eternal hills, nor reflected, as I tramped, upon the strange ways of man.

Oh, my friend, is it the settled rule of life that we are to accept nothing not expensive? It is not so settled for me; that which is freest, cheapest, seems somehow more valuable than anything I pay for; that which is given better than that which is bought; that which passes between you and me in the glance of an eye, a touch of the hand, is better than minted money!

I found Horace upon the March day I speak of just coming out of his new fruit cellar. Horace is a progressive and energetic man, a leader in this community, and the first to have a modern fruit cellar. By this means he ministers profitably to that appetite of men which craves most sharply that which is hardest to obtain: he supplies the world with apples in March.

It being a mild and sunny day, the door of the fruit cellar was open, and as I came around the corner I had such of whiff of fragrance as I cannot describe. It seemed as though the vials of the earth's most precious odours had been broken there in Horace's yard! The smell of ripe apples!

In the dusky depths of the cellar, down three steps, I could see Horace's ruddy face.

"How are ye, David," said he. "Will ye have a Good Apple?"

So he gave me a good apple. It was a yellow Bellflower without a blemish, and very large and smooth. The body of it was waxy yellow, but on the side where the sun had touched it, it blushed a delicious deep red. Since October it had been in the dark, cool storage-room, and Horace, like some old monkish connoisseur of wines who knows just when to bring up the bottles of a certain vintage, had chosen the exact moment in all the year when the vintage of the Bellflower was at its best. As he passed it to me I caught, a scent as of old crushed apple blossoms, or fancied I did or it may have been the still finer aroma of friendship which passed at the touching of our fingers.

It was a hand-filling apple and likewise good for tired eyes, an antidote for winter, a remedy for sick souls.

"A wonderful apple!" I said to Horace, holding it off at arm's length.

"No better grown anywhere," said he, with scarcely restrained pride.

I took my delight of it more nearly; and the odour was like new-cut clover in an old orchard, or strawberry leaves freshly trod upon, or the smell of peach wood at the summer pruning--how shall one describe it? at least a compound or essence of all the good odours of summer.

"Shall I eat it?" I asked myself, for I thought such a perfection of nature should be preserved for the blessing of mankind. As I hesitated, Horace remarked:

"It was grown to be eaten."

So I bit into it, a big liberal mouthful, which came away with a rending sound such as one hears sometimes in a winter's ice-pond. The flesh within, all dewy with moisture, was like new cream, except a rim near the surface where the skin had been broken; here it was of a clear, deep yellow.

New odours came forth and I knew for the first time how perfect in deliciousness such an apple could be. A mild, serene, ripe, rich bouquet, compounded essence of the sunshine from these old Massachusetts hills, of moisture drawn from our grudging soil, of all the peculiar virtues of a land where the summers make up in the passion of growth for the long violence of winter; the compensatory aroma of a life triumphant, though hedged about by severity, was in the bouquet of this perfect Bellflower. Like some of the finest of wines and the warmest of friends it was of two flavours, and was not to be eaten for mere nourishment, but was to be tasted and enjoyed. The first of the flavours came readily in a sweetness, richness, a slight acidity, that it might not cloy; but the deeper, more delicate flavour came later--if one were not crudely impatient--and was, indeed, the very soul of the fruit. One does not quickly arrive at souls either in apples or in friends. And I said to Horace with solemnity, for this was an occasion not to be lightly treated:

"I have never in my life tasted a fine apple."

"There is no finer apple," said Horace with conviction.

With that we fell to discussing the kinds and qualities of all the apples grown this side China, and gave our more or less slighting opinions of Ben Davises and Greenings and Russets, and especially of trivial summer apples of all sorts, and came to the conclusion at last that it must have been just after God created this particular "tree yielding fruit" that he desisted from his day's work and remarked that what he saw was good. The record is silent upon the point, and Moses is not given to adjectives, but I have often wondered what He would have said if He had not only seen the product of His creation, but *tasted* it.

I forgot to say that when I would have slurred the excellence of the Baldwin in comparison with the Bellflower, Horace began at once to interpose objections, and defended the excellence and perfection of that variety.

...He has fifty barrels of Baldwins in his cellar.

While we talked with much enjoyment of the lore of apples and apple-growing, I finished the Bellflower to the very core, and said to Horace as I reluctantly tossed aside the stem and three seeds:

"Surely this has been one of the rare moments of life."

CHAPTER IX
I GO TO THE CITY.

Surely man is a wonderfull, vaine, divers and wavering subject: It is very hard to * ground and directly constant and uniforme judgement upon him."

Though I live most of the time in the country, as I love best to do, sometimes I go to the city and find there much that is strange and amusing. I like to watch the inward flow of the human tide in the morning, and the ebb at evening, and sometimes in the slack tide of noon I drift in one of the eddies where the restless life of the city pauses a moment to refresh itself. One of the eddies I like best of all is near the corner of Madison Square, where the flood of Twenty-third Street swirls around the bulkhead of the Metropolitan tower to meet the transverse currents of Madison Avenue. Here, of a bright morning when Down-at-Heels is generously warming himself on the park benches, and Old Defeat watches Young Hurry striding by, one has a royal choice of refreshment: a "red-hot" enfolded in a bun from the dingy sausage wagon at the curb, or a plum for a penny from the Italian with the trundle cart, or news of the world in lurid gulps from the noon edition of the paper--or else a curious idea or so flung out stridently over the heads of the crowd by a man on a soap box.

I love this corner of the great city; I love the sense of the warm human tide flowing all about me. I love to look into the strange, dark, eager, sensitive, blunt faces.

The other noon, drifting there in that human eddy, I stopped to listen to a small, shabby man who stood in transitory eminence upon his soap box, half his body reaching above the knobby black soil of human heads around him--black, knobby soil that he was seeking, there in the spring sunshine, to plough with strange ideas. He had ruddy cheeks and a tuft of curly hair set like an upholstery button on each side of his bald head. The front teeth in his upper jaw were missing, and as he opened his mouth one could see the ample lining of red flannel.

He raised his voice penetratingly to overcome the noise of the world, straining until the dark-corded veins of his throat stood out sharply and perspiration gleamed on his bald forehead. As though his life depended upon the delivery of his great message he was explaining to that close-packed crowd that there was no God.

From time to time he offered for sale pamphlets by R.G. Ingersoll and Frederic Harrison, with grimy back numbers of a journal called the "Truth-Seeker."

By the slant and timbre of his speech he was an Englishman; he had a gift of vigorous statement, and met questioners like an intellectual pugilist with skilful blows between the eyes: and his grammar was bad.

I stood for some time listening to him while he proved with excellent logic, basing his reasoning on many learned authorities, that there was no God. His audience cheered with glee his clever hits, and held up their hands for the books he had for sale.

"Who is this speaker?" I asked the elbowing helper who came through the crowd to deliver the speaker's wares and collect the silver for them. "Who is this speaker who says there is no God?"

"Henry Moore," he responded.

"And who," I asked, "is Henry Moore?"

"He is an Englishman and was brought up a Presbyterian--but he seen the light."

"And no longer thinks there is any God?"

"Nope."

"And these books prove the same thing?"

"Yep."

So I bought one of them, thinking it wonderful that proof of so momentous a conclusion could be had for so small a sum.

This Henry Moore could fling arguments like thunderbolts; he could marshall his authorities like an army; he could talk against the roar of the city and keep his restless audience about him; and if he did not believe in God he had complete faith in Haeckel and Jacques Loeb, and took at face value the lightest utterances of John Stuart Mill.

I enjoyed listening to Henry Moore. I enjoyed looking into the faces all around me--mostly keen foreign or half-foreign faces, and young faces, and idle faces, and curious faces, and faces that drank in, and faces that disdainfully rejected.

After a time, however, I grew unaccountably weary of the vehemence of Henry Moore and of the adroit helper who hawked his books. And suddenly I looked up into the clear noon blue of the ancient sky. A pigeon was flying across the wide open spaces of the square, the sunlight glinting on its wings. I saw the quiet green tops of the trees in the park, and the statue of Roscoe Conkling, turning a nonchalant shoulder toward the heated speaker who said there was no God. How many strange ideas, contradictory arguments, curious logic, have fallen, this last quarter century, upon the stony ears of Roscoe Conkling! Far above me the Metropolitan tower, that wonder work of men, lifted itself grandly to the heavens, and all about I suddenly heard and felt the roar and surge of the mighty city, the mighty, careless, busy city, thousands of people stirring about me, souls full of hot hopes and mad desires, unsatisfied longings, unrealized ideals. And I stepped out of the group who were gathered around the man who said there was no God....

But I still drifted in the eddy, thinking how wonderful and strange all these things were, and came thus to another group, close gathered at the curb. It was much smaller than the other, and at the centre stood a patriarchal man with a white beard, and with him two women. He was leaning against the iron railing of the park, and several of the free-thinker's audience, freshly stuffed with arguments, had engaged him hotly. Just as I approached he drew from his pocket a worn, leather-covered Bible, and said, tapping it with one finger:

"For forty years I have carried this book with me. It contains more wisdom than any other book in the world. Your friend there can talk until he is hoarse--it will do no harm--but the world will continue to follow the wisdom of this book."

A kind of exaltation gleamed in his eye, and he spoke with an earnestness equal to that of Henry Moore. He, too, was a street speaker, waiting with his box at his side to begin. He would soon be standing up there to prove, also with logic and authority, that there was a God. He, also, would plough that knobby black soil of human heads with the share of his vehement faith. The two women were with him to sing their belief, and one had a basket to take up a collection, and the other, singling me out as I listened with eagerness, gave me a printed tract, a kind of advertisement of God.

I looked at the title of it. It was called: "God in His World."

"Does this prove that God is really in the world?" I asked.

"Yes," she said. "Will you read it?"

"Yes," I said, "I am glad to get it. It is wonderful that so great a truth can he established in so small a pamphlet, and all for nothing."

She looked at me curiously, I thought, and I put the tract by the side of the pamphlet I had bought from the freethinker, and drifted again in the eddy.

The largest crowd of all was close packed about a swarthy young chap whose bushy hair waved in response to the violence of his oratory. He, too, was perspiring with his ideas. He had a marvellous staccato method of question and answer. He would shoot a question like a rifle bullet at the heads of his audience, and then stiffen back like a wary boxer, both clenched hands poised in a tremulous gesticulation, and before any one could answer his bullet-like question, he was answering it himself. As I edged my way nearer to him I discovered that he, also, had a little pile of books at his feet which a keen-eyed assistant was busily selling. How well-established the technic of this art of the city eddies! How well-studied the psychology!

I thought this example the most perfect of them all, and watched with eagerness the play of the argument as it was mirrored in the intent faces all about me. And gradually I grew interested in what the man was saying, and thought of many good answers I could give to his questionings if he were not so cunning with answers of his own. Finally, in the midst of one of his loftiest flights, he demanded, hotly:

"Are you not, every one of you, a slave of the capitalist class?"

It was perfectly still for a second after he spoke, and before I knew what I was doing, I responded:

"Why, no, I'm not."

It seemed to astonish the group around me: white faces turned my way.

But it would have been difficult to dash that swarthy young man. He was as full of questions as a porcupine is full of quills.

"Well, sir," said he, "if I can prove to you that you are a slave, will you believe it?"

"No," I said, "unless you make me feel like a slave, too! No man is a slave who does not feel slavish."

But I was no match for that astonishing young orator; and he had the advantage over me of a soap box! Moreover, at that moment, the keen-eyed assistant, never missing an opportunity, offered me one of his little red books.

"If you can read this without feeling a slave," he remarked, "you're John D. himself in disguise."

I bought his little red book and put it with the pamphlet of the freethinker, and the tract of the God-fearing man, and stepped out of that group, feeling no more servile than when I went in. And I said to myself:

"This, surely, is a curious place to be in."

For I was now strangely interested in these men of the eddy.

"There are more gods preached here," I said, "than ever were known on the Acropolis."

Up the square a few paces I saw a covered wagon with a dense crowd around it. And in front of it upon a little platform which raised the speaker high above the heads of the audience stood a woman, speaking with shrill ardour. Most of the hearers were men; and she was telling them with logic and authority that the progress of civilization waited upon the votes of women. The army of the world stood still until the rear rank of its women could be brought into line! Morals languished, religion faded, industries were brutalized, home life destroyed! If only women had their rights the world would at once become a beautiful and charming place! Oh, she was a powerful and earnest speaker; she made me desire above everything, at the first opportunity, to use my share of the power in this Government to provide each woman with a vote. And just as I had reached this compliant stage there came a girl smiling and passing her little basket. The sheer art of it! So I dropped in my coin and took the little leaflet she gave me and put it side by side with the other literature of my accumulating library.

And so I came away from those hot little groups with their perspiring orators, and felt again the charm of the tall buildings and the wide sunny square, and the park with Down-at-Heels warming his ragged shanks, and the great city clanging heedlessly by. How serious they all were there in their eddies! Is there no God? Will woman suffrage or socialism cure all the evils of this mad world which, ill as it is, we would not be without? Is a belief for forty years in the complete wisdom of the Book the final solution? Why do not all of the seeking and suffering thousands flowing by in Twenty-third Street stop here in the eddies to seek the solution of their woes, the response to their hot desires?

So I came home to the country, thinking of what I had seen and heard, asking myself, "What is the truth, after all? What *is* real?"

And I was unaccountably glad to be at home again. As I came down the hill through the town road the valley had a quiet welcome for me, and the trees I know best, and the pleasant fields of corn and tobacco, and the meadows ripe with hay. I know of nothing more comforting to the questioning spirit than the sight of distant hills....

I found that Bill had begun the hay cutting. I saw him in the lower field as I came by in the road. There he was, stationed high on the load, and John, the Pole, was pitching on. When he saw me he lifted one arm high in the air and waved his hand--and I in return gave him the sign of the Free Fields.

"Harriet," I said, "it seems to me I was never so glad before to get home."

"It's what you always say," she remarked placidly.

"This time it's true!" And I put the pamphlets I had accumulated in the city eddies upon the pile of documents which I fully intend to read but rarely get to.

The heavenly comfort of an old shirt! The joy of an old hat!

As I walked down quickly into the field with my pitchfork on my shoulder to help Bill with the hay, I was startled to see, hanging upon a peach tree at the corner of the orchard, a complete suit of black clothes. Near it, with the arms waving gently in the breeze, was a white shirt and a black tie, and at the foot of the tree a respectable black hat. It was as though the peach tree had suddenly, on that bright day, gone into mourning.

I laughed to myself.

"Bill," I said, "what does this mean?"

Bill is a stout jolly chap with cheeks that look, after half a day's haying, like raw beef-steaks. He paused on his load, smiling broadly, his straw hat set like a halo on the back of his head.

"Expected a funeral," he said cheerfully.

Bill is the undertaker's assistant, and is always on call in cases of emergency.

"What happened, Bill?"

"They thought they'd bury 'im this afternoon, but they took an' kep' 'im over till to-morrow."

"But you came prepared."

"Yas, no time to go home in hayin'. The pump fer me, and the black togs."

Bill calls the first rakings of the hay "tumbles," and the scattered re-rakings, which he despises, he calls "scratchings." I took one side of the load and John, the Pole, the other and we put on great forkfuls from the tumbles which Bill placed skilfully at the corners and sides of the load, using the scratchings for the centre.

John, the Pole, watched the load from below. "Tank he too big here," he would say, or, "Tank you put more there"; but Bill told mostly by the feel of the load under his feet or by the "squareness of his eye." John, the Pole, is a big, powerful fellow, and after smoothing down the load with his fork he does not bother to rake up the combings, but gathering a bunch of loose hay with his fork, he pushes it by main strength, and very quickly, around the load, and running his fork through the heap, throws it upon the mountain-high load in a twinkling--an admirable, deft performance.

Hay-making is a really beautiful process: the clicking mower cutting its clean, wide swath, a man stepping after, where the hay is very heavy, to throw the wind-row back a little. Then, after lying to wilt and dry in the burning sun--all full of good odours--the horse-rake draws it neatly into wide billows, and after that, John, the Pole, and I roll the billows into tumbles. Or, if the hay is slow in drying, as it was not this year, the kicking tedder goes over it, spreading it widely. Then the team and rack on the smooth-cut meadow and Bill on the load, and John and I pitching on; and the talk and badinage that goes on, the excitement over disturbed field mice, the discussion of the best methods of killing woodchucks, tales of marvellous exploits of loaders and stackers, thrilling incidents of the wet year of '98 when two men and one team saved four acres of hay by working all night--"with lanterns, I jing"--much talk of how she goes on, "she" being the hay, and no end of observations upon the character, accomplishments, faults, and excesses of the sedate old horses waiting comfortably out in front, half hidden by the mountain of hay above them and nibbling at the tumbles as they go by.

Then the proud moment when Bill the driver, with legs apart, almost pushing on the reins, drives his horses up the hill.

"Go it, Dick. Let 'er out, Daisy. Stiddy, ol' boy. Whoa, there. Ease down now. Hey, there, John, block the wheel--block the wheel I tell ye. Ah-h now, jes' breathe a bit. I jing, it's hot."

And then the barn, the cavernous dark doors, the hoofs of the horses thundering on the floor, the smell of cattle from below, the pigeons in the loft whirring startled from their perches. Then the hot, scented, dusty "pitching off" and "mowing in"--a fine process, an **honest** process: men sweating for what they get.

As I came in from the field that night the sun was low in the hills, and a faint breeze had begun to blow, sweetly cool after the burning heat of the day. And I felt again that curious deep sense I have so often here in the country, of the soundness and reality of the plain things of life.

CHAPTER X
THE OLD STONE MASON

Of well-flavoured men, I know none better than those who live close to the soil or work in common things. Men are like roses and lilacs, which, too carefully cultivated to please the eye, lose something of their native fragrance. One of the best-flavoured men I know is my friend, the old stone mason.

To-day I rode over with the old stone mason to select some wide stones for steps in my new building. The old man loves stones. All his life long--he is now beyond seventy years old--he has lived among stones, lifted stones, fitted stones. He knows all the various kinds, shapes, sizes, and where they will go best in a wall. He can tell at a glance where to strike a stone to make it fit a particular place, and out of a great pile he can select with a shrewd eye the stone for the exact opening he has to fill. He will run his stubby rough hand over a stone and remark:

"Fine face that. Ye don't see many such stones these days," as though he were speaking of the countenance of a friend.

I veritably believe there are stones that smile at him, stones that frown at him, stones that appear good or ill-humoured to him as he bends his stocky strong body to lift or lay them. He is a slow man, a slow, steady, geologic man, as befits one who works with the elemental stuff of nature. His arms are short and his hands powerful. He has been a servant of stones in this neighbourhood alone for upward of fifty years.

He loves stones and can no more resist a good stone than I a good book. When going about the country, if he sees comely stones in a wayside pile, or in a fine-featured old fence he will have them, whether or no, and dickers for them with all the eagerness, sly pride, and half-concealed cunning with which a lover of old prints chaffers for a Seymour Haden in a second-hand book shop. And when he has bought them he takes the first idle day he has, and with his team of old horses goes into the hills, or wherever it may be, and brings them down. He has them piled about his barn and even in his yard, as another man might have flower beds. And he can tell you, as he told me to-day, just where a stone of such a size and such a face can be found, though it be at the bottom of a pile. No book lover with a feeling sense for the place in his cases where each of his books may be found has a sharper instinct than he. In his pocket he carries a lump of red chalk, and when we had made our selections he marked each stone with a broad red cross.

I think it good fortune that I secured the old stone mason to do my work, and take to myself some credit for skill in enticing him. He is past seventy years old, though of a ruddy fresh countenance and a clear bright eye, and takes no more contracts, and is even reluctantly persuaded to do the ordinary stone work of the neighbourhood. He is "well enough off," as the saying goes, to rest during the remainder of his years, for he has lived a temperate and frugal life, owns his own home with the little garden behind it, and has money in the bank. But he can be prevailed upon, like an old artist who has reached the time of life when it seems as important to enjoy as to create, he can sometimes be prevailed upon to lay a wall for the joy of doing it.

So I had the stone hauled onto the ground, the best old field stone I could find, and I had a clean, straight foundation dug, and when all was ready I brought the old man over to look at it. I said I wanted his advice. No sooner did his glance light upon the stone, no sooner did he see the open and ready earth than a new light came in his eye. His step quickened and as he went about he began to hum an old tune under his breath. I knew then that I had him! He had taken fire. I could see that his eye was already selecting the stones that should "go down," the fine square stones to make the corners or cap the wall, and measuring with a true eye the number of little stones for the fillers. In no time at all he had agreed to do my work; indeed, would have felt aggrieved if I had not employed him.

I enjoyed the building of the wall, I think, as much as he did, and helped him what I could by rolling the larger stones close down to the edge of the wall. As the old man works he talks, if any one cares to listen, or if one does not care to listen he is well content to remain silent among his stones. But I enjoyed listening, for nothing in this world is so fascinating to me as the story of how a man has come to be what he is. When we think of it there are no abstract adventures in this world, but only your adventure and my adventure, and it is only as we come to know a man that we can see how wonderful his life has been.

He told me all about the great walls and the little walls--miles and miles of them--he has built in the course of fifty years. He told of crude boyhood walls when he was a worker for wages only, he told of proud manhood walls when he took contracts for foundations, retaining walls, and even for whole buildings, such as churches, where the work was mostly of stone; he told me of thrilling gains and profits, and of depressing losses; and he told me of his calm later work, again on wages, for which he is chosen as a master of his craft. A whole long lifetime of it-- and the last years the best of all!

As we drove up yesterday to select the steps from his piles of old field stone, riding behind his great, slow, hairy-hoofed horse, in the battered and ancient wagon, he pointed with his stubby whip to this or that foundation, the work of his hands.

"Fine job, that," said he, and I looked for the first time in my life at the beautiful stonework beneath the familiar home of a friend. I had seen the house a thousand times, and knew well the people in it, but my unobservant eye had never before rested consciously upon that bit of basement wall. How we go through life, losing most of the beauties of it from sheer inability to see! But the old man, as he drives about, rarely sees houses at all, especially wooden houses, and for all modern stucco and cement work he entertains a kind of lofty contempt. Sham work of a hasty and unskilled age! He never, I think, put in a shovelful of cement except in the place where it belongs, as a mortar for good walls, and never will do so as long as he lives. So long as he lives the standards of high art will never be debased!

He built that foundation, and this chimney, he worked on the tower of the Baptist church in the town, "and never yet has there been a crack in her, winter or summer"; and more than forty years ago he laid the cornerstone of the old schoolhouse, the foundation walls of which stand to-day as sound and strong as they were when they were put down.

In dry walls I think the old stone mason takes the greatest pride of all: for it is in the dry wall--I mean by that a wall laid without mortar--that the sheer art of the mason comes most into play. Any one can throw a wall together if he has mortar to make it stick, but a dry wall must stand out for what it is, built solid from the bottom up, each stone resting securely upon those below it, and braced and nested in by the sheer skill of the mason. The art of the dry wall is the ancient heritage of New England and speaks not only of the sincerity and the conscientiousness of the old Puritan spirit but strikes the higher note of beauty. Many of the older walls I know are worth going far to see, for they exhibit a rare sense of form and proportion, and are sometimes set in the landscape with a skill that only the Master-Artist himself could exceed. Those old, hard-wrought stone fences of the Burnham Hills and Crewsbury, the best of them, were honestly built, and built to last a thousand years. A beautiful art--and one that is passing away! It is the dry wall that stands of itself that the old stone mason loves best of all.

As we drove along the road the old man pointed out to me with his stubby whip so many examples of his work that it seemed finally as if he had borne a hand in nearly everything done in this neighbourhood in the last half-century. He has literally built himself into the country and into the town, and at seventy years of age he can look back upon it all with honest pride. It stands. No jerry-work anywhere. No cracks. It stands.

I never realized before how completely the neighbourhood rests upon the work of this simple old man. He *founded* most of the homes here, and upon his secure walls rest many of the stores, the churches, and the schools of the countryside. I see again how important each man is to the complete fabric of civilization and know that we are to leave no one out, despise no one, look down upon no one.

He told me stories of this ancient settler and of that.

He was a powerful queer man--he wanted the moss left on his stones when I put 'em in; never a hammer touched the facings of *his* wall...

"That is properly a woman's wall. She was the boss, you might call it, and wanted stone, but *he* wanted brick. So you see the front, where people can see it, is of stone, but the sides is all brick."

Thus like the true artist that he is, he has not only built himself his own honesty, truth, skill, into the town, but he has built in the inexhaustible peculiarities, the radiant charm, the hates and the loves, of the people of this place. He has mirrored his own little age in stone. He knows the town, indeed, better than most of us, having a kind of stone-age knowledge of it--the fundamental things men build in when they set about building permanently.

"And that is what you might call a spite-wall," said he, showing me a long wall leading between two shady homes, making one of them a prison on the south, and the other a prison on the north. He told me the story of an ancient and bitter quarrel between two old friends, a story which sounded to-day among spring blossoms like the account of some ancient baronial feud.

But if the old stone mason has built walls to keep enemies apart how many more walls has he built to keep friends together? How many times has he been consulted by shy lovers seeking a foundation for a new home, a new family, how many times by Darby and Joan planning a resting place for the sunny closing years of their lives! He could point, indeed, to one wall that symbolized hatred; all the others meant homes, roof-trees, families, or they were the foundations for the working places of men, or else, like the tower of the church, they pointed heavenward and were built to the glory of God.

The old stone mason has not the slightest idea that he has done anything unusual or wonderful. He is as simple and honest a man as ever I knew; and if he has pride, simple and honest also in that. He was anxious not to charge me too much for the stone I bought--in an age like this! I have never talked with him about God, or about religion: I had no need to.

He has done his duty in other ways by his time and his place. He has brought up a large family of children; and has known sorrow and loss, as well as happiness and contentment. Two of his children were taken in one day with pneumonia. He told me about it with a quaver in his old voice.

"How long ago was it?" I asked.

"Twenty-seven years."

He has sons and daughters left, and two of the sons he has well trained as stone masons after him. They are good as young men go in a degenerate age. They insist on working in cement! He has grandchildren in school, and spoils them.

He is also a man of public interests and upon town-meeting day puts on his good clothes and sits modestly toward the back of the hall. Though he rarely says anything he always has a strong opinion, an opinion as sound and hard as stones and as simple, upon most of the questions that come up. And he votes as he thinks, though the only man in meeting who votes that way. For when a man works in the open, laying walls true to lines and measurements, being honest with natural things, he comes clear, sane, strong, upon many things. I would sooner trust his judgment upon matters that are really important as between man and man, and man and God, than I would trust the town lawyer. And if he has grown a little testy with some of the innovations of modern life, and thinks they did everything better forty years ago--and says so--he speaks, at least, his honest conviction.

If I can lay my walls as true as he does, if I can build myself a third part as firmly into any neighbourhood as he has into this, if at seventy years of age--if ever I live to lay walls with joy at that time of life--if I can look back upon *my* foundations, *my* heaven-pointing towers, and find no cracks or strains in them, I shall feel that I have made a great success of my life....

I went out just now: the old man was stooping to lift a heavy stone. His hat was off and the full spring sunshine struck down warmly upon the ruddy bald spot on the top of his head, the white hair around about it looking silvery in that light. As he placed the stone in the wall, he straightened up and rubbed his stubby hand along it.

"A fine stone that!" said he.

CHAPTER XI
AN AUCTION OF ANTIQUES

"I would not paint a face
  Or rocks or streams or trees
Mere semblances of things--
  But something more than these."

"I would not play a tune
  Upon the sheng or lute
Which did not also sing
  Meanings that else were mute."

John Templeton died on the last day of August, but it was not until some weeks later that his daughter Julida, that hard-favoured woman, set a time for the auction. It fell happily upon a mellow autumn day, and as I drove out I saw the apples ripening in all the orchards along the road, and the corn was beginning to look brown, and the meadows by the brook were green with rowen. It was an ideal day for an auction, and farmers and townsmen came trooping from all parts of the country, for the Templeton antiques were to be sold.

John Templeton lived in one house for seventy-eight years; he was born there, and you will find the like of that in few places in America. It was a fine house for its time, for any time, and not new when John Templeton was born. A great, solid, square structure, such as they built when the Puritan spirit was virile in New England, with an almost Greek beauty of measured lines. It has a fanlight over the front door, windows exquisitely proportion, and in the center a vast brick chimney. Even now, though weathered and unpainted, it stands four-square upon the earth with a kind of natural dignity. A majestic chestnut tree grows near it, and a large old barn and generous sheds, now somewhat dilapidated, ramble away to the rear.

Enclosing the fields around about are stone fences representing the infinite labour of John Templeton's forebears. More toil has gone into the stone fences of New England, free labour of a free people, than ever went into the slave-driven building of the Pyramids of Egypt.

I knew John Templeton in his old age--a stiff, weather-beaten old man driving to town in a one-horse buggy.

"How are you, Mr. Templeton?"

"Comin' on, comin' on." This was his invariable reply.

He had the old New England pronunciation, now disappearing. He said "rud" for road, "daown" for down, and gave an indescribable twist to the word garden, best spelled "gardin." He had also the old New England ways. He was forehanded with his winter woodpile, immaculately neat with his dooryard, determined in his Sunday observance, and if he put the small apples in the middle of the barrel he refused to raise tobacco, lest it become a cause of stumbling to his neighbour. He paid his debts, disciplined his children, and in an age which has come to look chummily upon God, he dreaded His wrath.

He grew a peculiar, very fine variety of sweet apple which I have never seen anywhere else. He called it the Pumpkin Sweet, for it was of a rich yellow. I can see him yet, driving into town with a shallow wagon box half full of this gold of the orchard; can see him turn stiffly to get one of the apples for me; can hear him say in the squeaky voice of age:

"Ye won't find no sweeter apples hereabout, I can tell ye that."

He was a dyed-in-the-wool abolition Republican and took the Boston *Transcript* for forty-six years. He left two cords of them piled up in a back storeroom. He loved to talk about Napoleon Bonaparte and the Battle of Waterloo, and how, if there had not been that delay of half an hour, the history of the world might have been different. I can see him saying, with the words puffing out his loose cheeks:

"And then Blooker kem up--"

To the very last, even when his eyes were too dim to read and his voice was cracked, he would start up, like some old machine set a-whirring when you touched the rusty lever, and talk about the Battle of Waterloo.

No one, so far as I know, ever heard him complain, or bemoan his age, or regret the change in the times; and when his day came, he lay down upon his bed and died.

"Positively nothing will be reserved," were the familiar words of the poster, and they have a larger meaning in an old country neighbourhood than the mere sale of the last pan and jug and pig and highboy. Though we live with our neighbours for fifty years we still secretly wonder about them. We still suspect that something remains covered, something kept in and hidden away, some bits of beauty unappreciated--as they are, indeed, with ourselves. But death snatches away the last friendly garment of concealment; and after the funeral the auction. We may enter now. The doors stand at last flung widely open; all the attics have been ransacked; all the chests have been turned out; a thousand privacies stand glaringly revealed in the sunny open spaces of the yard. Positively nothing will be reserved; everything will be knocked down to the highest bidder. What wonder that the neighbourhood gathers, what wonder that it nods its head, leaves sentences half uttered, smiles enigmatically.

Nearly all the contents of the house had been removed to the yard, under the great chestnut tree. A crowd of people, mostly women, were moving about among the old furniture, the old furniture that had been in John Templeton's family for no one knows how long--old highboys and lowboys, a beautifully simple old table or so, and beds with carved posts, and hand-wrought brasses, and an odd tall clock that struck with sonorous dignity. These things, which had been temptingly advertised as "antiques," a word John Templeton never knew, were only the common serviceable things of uncounted years of family life.

Nothing about the place was of any great value except the antiques, and it was these that drew the well-dressed women in automobiles from as far away as Hempfield and Nortontown; and yet there were men in plenty to poke the pigs, look sarcastically at the teeth of the two old horses, and examine with calculating and rather jeering eyes John Templeton's ancient buggy, and the harness and the worn plough and cultivator and mowing machine. Everything seems so cheap, so poor, so unprotected, when the spirit has departed.

Under the chestnut tree the swarthy auctioneer with his amiable countenance and ironical smile acquired through years of dispassionate observation of the follies of human emotion, the mutability of human affairs, the brevity of human endeavour, that brought everything at last under his hammer--there by the chestnut tree the auctioneer had taken his stand in temporary eminence upon an old chest, with an ancient kitchen cupboard near him which served at once as a pulpit for exhortation, and a block for execution. Already the well-worn smile had come pat to his countenance, and the well-worn witticisms were ready to his tongue.

"Now, gentlemen, if you'll give me such attention as you can spare from the ladies, we have here to-day----"

But I could not, somehow, listen to him: the whole scene, the whole deep event, had taken hold upon me strangely. It was so full of human meaning, human emotion, human pathos. I drifted away from the crowd and stepped in at the open door of the old house, and walked through the empty, resounding rooms with their curious old wallpaper and low ceilings and dusty windows. And there were the old fireplaces where the heavy brick had been eaten away by the pokings and scrapings of a century; and the thresholds worn by the passage of many feet, the romping feet of children, the happy feet of youth the bride passed here on her wedding night with her arm linked in the arm of the groom; the sturdy, determined feet of maturity; the stumbling feet of old age creeping in; the slow, pushing feet of the bearers with the last burden, crowding out--

The air of the house had a musty, shut-in odour, ironically cut through, as all old things are, by the stinging odour of the new: the boiling of the auction coffee in the half-dismantled kitchen, the epochal moment in the life of Julia Templeton. I could hear, occasionally, her high, strident worried voice ordering a helper about. Such a hard-favoured woman!

It is the studied and profitable psychology of the auction that the rubbish must be sold first--pots and bottles and jugs at five-cent bids, and hoes at ten--and after that, the friction of the contest having warmed in the bidders an amiable desire to purchase goods they do not want and cannot use, the auctioneer gradually puts forth the treasures of the day.

As I came out of the old house I could see that the mystic web had been spun, that the great moment of the sale was arriving. The auctioneer was leaning forward now upon the tall cupboard with an air of command, and surveying the assembled crowd with a lordly eye.

"Now, Jake, careful there--pass it along--steady.... We come now to the cheff dooves of the day, the creem delly creems of this sale. Gentleman *and* ladies, it is a great moment in the life of an auctioneer when he can offer, for sale, free and without reservation, such treasures as these...."

I could feel the warming interest of the crowd gathering in more closely about Mr. Harpworth, the furtive silences of shrewd bargainers, eagerness masked as indifference, and covetousness cloaking itself with smiling irony. It is in the auction that trade glorifies itself finally as an Art.

"Here, gentlemen *and* ladies, is a genuine antique, hand-wrought and solid all the way through. Just enough worn to give the flavour and distinction of age. Well built in the first place, plain, simple lines, but, ladies, ***beautiful***."

It was the tall four-post bed he was selling and he now put his hand upon this object--a hardy service with a cunningly simulated air of deference. It was to be profaned by no irreverent handling!

"What am I offered for this heirloom of the Templeton family? Ten? Ten! Fifteen over there, thank you, Mr. Cody. Why, gentlemen, that bed cannot be duplicated in America! A real product of Colonial art! Look at the colour of it! Where will you find such depth of colour in any modern piece? Age varnished it, gentlemen, age and use--the use of a hundred years.... Twenty over there, twenty I hear, twenty, twenty, make it thirty.... Speak up now, Ike, we know you've come here to-day to make your fortune--do I hear thirty?"

No sooner had the great bed been sold ("it's yours, Mrs. Craigie, a treasure and dirt cheap") there came an ancient pair of hand-wrought andirons, and a spider-legged table, and a brass warming-pan, and a banjo clock....

I scarcely know how to explain it, but the sale of these inanimate antiques, so charged with the restrained grace, the reticent beauty, the serviceable strength, of a passing age, took hold upon me with strange intensity. In times of high emotion the veil between sight and insight slips aside and that which lies about us suddenly achieves a higher reality. We are conscious of

"Something beside the form Something beyond the sound."

It came to me with a thrill that this was no mere sale of antique wood and brass and iron, but a veritable auction, here symbolized, of the decaying fragments of a sternly beautiful civilization.

I looked off across the stony fields, now softly green in the sunlight, from which three generations of the Templeton family had wrung an heroic living; I looked up at the majestic old house where they had lived and married and died....

As my eye came back to the busy scene beneath the chestnut tree it seemed to me, how vividly I cannot describe--that beside or behind the energetic and perspiring Mr. Harpworth there stood Another Auctioneer. And I thought he had flowing locks and a patriarchal beard, and a scythe for a sign of the uncertainty of life, and a glass to mark the swiftness of its passage. He was that Great Auctioneer who brings all things at last under his inexorable hammer.

After that, though Mr. Harpworth did his best, he claimed my attention only intermittently from that Greater Sale which was going on at his side, from that Greater Auctioneer who was conducting it with such consummate skill--for *he* knew that nothing is for sale but life. The mahogany highboy, so much packed and garnered life cut into inanimate wood; the andirons, so much life; the bookshelves upon which John Templeton kept his "Life of Napoleon Bonaparte," so much life. Life for sale, gentlemen! What am I offered to-day for this bit of life--and this--and this--

Mr. Harpworth had paused, for even an auctioneer, in the high moment of his art, remains human; and in the silence following the cessation of the metallic click of his voice, "Thirty, thirty, thirt, thirt--make it thirty-five--thank you--forty," one could hear the hens gossiping in the distant yard.

"There were craftsmen in those days, gentlemen," he was resuming; "look at this example of their art--there is quality here and durability----"

At this point the Great Auctioneer broke in upon my attention and caught up Mr. Harpworth's words:

"Yes, quality and durability--quality and durability. I also have here to-day, and will offer you, gentlemen, a surpassing antique, not built of wood nor fashioned in brass or iron, but a thing long attached to these acres and this house. I present for your consideration the married life of John Templeton and Hannah his wife. They lived together forty years, and the record scarcely shows a dent. In all that time hardly a word of love passed between them; but never a word of hatred, either. They had a kind of hard and fast understanding, like the laws of Moses. He did the work of the fields and she did the work of the house, from sunrise to sunset. On Sunday they went to church together. He got out at five o'clock to milk and harness up; and it made double work for her, what with getting the children cleaned, and the milk taken care of, and the Sunday dinner made ready. But neither he nor she every doubted or complained. It was the Lord's way. She bore him eight children. She told him before the last one came that she was not equal to it.... After that she was an invalid for seventeen years until she died. And there was loss of children to bear between them, and sickness, and creeping age, but this bit of furniture held firm to the last. Gentlemen, it was mad solid, no veneer, a good job all the way through."

As he spoke I thought that his roving eye (perhaps it was only my own!) fell upon Johnny Holcomb, whose married life has been full of vicissitudes.

"John, take this home with you; *you* can use it."

"Nope, no such married life for me," I thought I could hear him responding, rather pleased than not to be the butt of the auctioneer.

"Do I hear any bids?" the Great Auctioneer was saying, almost in the words of Mr. Harpworth. "**What!** No one wants n married life like this? Well, put it aside, Jake. It isn't wanted. Too old-fashioned."

It was Julia Templeton herself who now appeared with certain of the intimate and precious "bedroom things"--a wonderful old linen bedspread, wrought upon with woollen figures, and exaling an ancient and exquisite odour of lavender, and a rag rug or so, and a little old rocking chair with chintz coverings in which more than one Templeton mother had rocked her baby to sleep. Julia herself----

I saw Julia, that hard-favoured woman, for the first time at that moment, really saw her. How fiercely she threw down the spread and the rugs! How bold and unweeping her eyes! How hard and straight the lines of her mouth!

"Here they are, Mr. Harpworth!"

How shrill her voice; and how quickly she turned back to the noisy kitchen! I could see the angular form, the streakings of gray in her hair. ...

"What am I offered now for this precious antique? This hand-made spread? Everything sold without reserve! Come, now, don't let this opportunity slip by." He leaned forward confidentially and persuasively: "Fellah citizens, styles change and fashions pass away, but things made like these, good lines, strong material, honest work, they never grow old...."

Here the Shadowy Auctioneer broke in again and lifted me out of that limited moment.

"A true word!" he was saying. "Styles change and fashions pass away, and only those things that are well made, and made for service the beautiful things remain. I am offering to-day, without reservation, another precious antique. What will you give for such a religious faith as that of John Templeton? Worn for a lifetime and sound to the end. He read the Bible every Sunday morning of his life, went to church, and did his religious duty by his children. Do you remember young Joe Templeton? Wouldn't learn his chapter one Sunday, and the old gentleman prayed about it and then beat him with a hitching strap. Joe ran away from home and made his fortune in Minnesota. Nearly broke the mother's heart, and old John's, too; but he thought it right, and never repented it. Gentlemen, an honest man who feared God and lived righteously all his days! What am I offered for this durable antique, this characteristic product of New England? Do I hear a bid?"

At this I felt coming over me that strange urge of the auction, to bid and to buy. A rare possession indeed, not without a high, stern kind of beauty! It would be wonderful to possess such a faith; but what had I to offer that Shadowy Auctioneer? What coin that would redeem past times and departed beliefs?

It was curious how the words of Mr. Harpworth fitted into the fabric of my imaginings. When he next attracted my attention he was throwing up his hands in a fine semblance of despair. We were such obtuse purchasers!

"I think," said Mr. Harpworth, "that this crowd came here to-day only to eat Julia Templeton's auction luncheon. What's the matter with this here generation? You don't want things that are well made and durable, but only things that are cheap and flashy. Put 'er aside, Jake. We'll sell 'er yet to some historical museum devoted to the habits and customs of the early Americans."

He was plainly disgusted with us, and we felt it keenly, and were glad and pleased when, a moment later, he gave evidence of being willing to go on with us, paltry as we were.

"Jake, pass up that next treasure."

His spirits were returning; his eyes gleamed approvingly upon the newly presented antique. He looked at us with fresh confidence; he was still hopeful that we would rise to his former good opinion of us.

"And now before I sell the hail clock by Willard, date of 1822, I am going to offer what is possibly the best single piece in this sale...."

Here again the Old Auctioneer, having caught his cue broke in. When he spoke, who could listen to Mr. Harpworth?

"... the best single piece in this sale, gentlemen! I offer you now the Templeton family pride! A choice product of old New England. A little battered, but still good and sound. The Templetons! They never did anything notable except to work, work early and late, summer and winter, for three generations. They were proud of any one who bore the Templeton name; they were proud even of Jim, simple Jim, who got a job driving the delivery wagon at the hill store, and drove it for twenty-two years and was drowned in Mill River. I'll tell you what family pride meant to old John Templeton...."

I thought he leaned forward to take us into his confidence, motioning at the same time toward the house.

"You know Julia Templeton----"

Know her? Of course we knew her! Knew her as only the country knows its own.

"When Julia ran away with that sewing-machine agent--it was her only chance!--old John Templeton drove his best cow into town and sold her, he mortgaged his team of horses, and went after the girl and brought her home with him. They were firm and strong and as righteous as God with her; and they paid off, without whining, the mortgages on the horses, and never spoke of the loss of the cow--but never forgot it. They held up their heads to the end. Gentlemen, what am I offered for this interesting antique, this rare work of art?"

*   *   *   *   *

The auction was considered, upon the whole, a great success. Mr. Harpworth himself said so. Ike, the Jewish dealer, bought the family clock and the spring-tooth harrow, and even bid on the family crayon portraits (the frames could be sold for something or other); a Swede bought the pigs and the old buggy; an Irish teamster bid in John Templeton's horses, and a Pole, a good man, I know him well, bought the land, and will no doubt keep his geese in the summer kitchen, and get rich from the cultivation of the ancient fields. While old John Templeton bowed himself humbly before a wrathful God he would never go down on his knees, as the Poles do, to the fertile earth. And--I forgot--an Italian from Nortontown bought for a song the apple and chestnut crops, and busy third generation Americans loaded in the antiques and drove off with them to the city.

The last I saw of Julia Templeton, that hard-favoured woman, she was standing, an angular figure, in the midst of the wreck of the luncheon dishes, one arm wrapped in her apron, the other hand shading her eyes while she watched the company, in wagons and automobiles, trailing away to the westward, and the towns....

The sale was over; but the most valuable antiques of all found no purchasers: they were left behind with Julia Templeton: only she could use them.

CHAPTER XII
A WOMAN OF FORTY-FIVE

We have an Astonishing Woman in this community. She acts in a way that no one expects, and while we are intensely interested in everything she does, and desire to know about it to the uttermost detail, we are inclined to speak of her in bated breath.

Some Woman to Talk About in a country neighbourhood is a kind of public necessity. She fills one of the stated functions like the town assessor, or the president of the Dorcas Society; and if ever the office falls vacant we have immediate resort to one of those silent elections at which we choose our town celebrities. There are usually several candidates, and the campaign is accompanied by much heated argument and exemplification. We have our staunch party men and our irresponsible independents on whom you can never put your finger; and if we are sometimes a little vague in our discussion of principles and issues we share with our national political leaders an intense interest in personalities. Prominent citizens "come out" for this candidate or that, we "spring surprises," and launch new booms, and often, at the last moment, we are taken off our feet by the circulation of comebacks. I take a pardonable pride, however, in saying, to the credit of our democratic institutions that most of the candidates elected are chosen strictly upon merit.

I shall never forget the afternoon, now more than a year ago, that Harriet came up the road bearing the news which, beyond a doubt, placed the present incumbent in office; and has served to keep her there, despite the efforts in certain quarters, which shall be nameless, to use that pernicious instrument of radicalism, the recall.

I can always tell when Harriet brings important news. She has a slightly quicker step, carries her head a little more firmly, and when she speaks impresses her message upon me with a lowered voice. When Harriet looks at me severely and drops down an octave I prepare for the worst.

"David," she said, "Mary Starkweather has gone to live in the barn!"

"In the **barn**!"

"In the barn."

I don't know quite why it is, but I dislike being surprised, and do my best to cover it up, and, besides, I have always liked Mary Starkweather. So I remarked, as casually as I could:

"Why not? It's a perfectly good barn."

"David Grayson!"

"Well, it is. It's a better building to-day than many of the people of this town live in. Why shouldn't Mary Starkweather live in the barn if she wants to? It's her barn."

"But, **David**--there are her children--and her husband!"

"There always are, when anybody wants to live in a barn."

"I shall not talk with you any more," said Harriet, "until you can be serious."

I had my punishment, as I richly deserved to have, in the gnawing of unsatis-fied curiosity, which is almost as distressing as a troubled conscience.

Within the next few days, I remember, I heard the great news buzzing every-where I went. We had conjectured that the barn was being refitted for the family of a caretaker, and it was Mary Starkweather herself, our sole dependable represen-tative of the Rich, who was moving in! Mary Starkweather, who had her house in town, and her home in the country, and her automobiles, and her servants, and her pictures, and her books, to say nothing of her husband and her children and her children's maid going to live in her barn! I leave it to you if there was not a valid reason for our commotion.

It must have been two weeks later that I went to town by the upper hill road in order to pass the Starkweather place. It is a fine old estate, the buildings, except the barn, set well back from the road with a spacious garden near them, and pleasant fields stretching away on every hand. As I skirted the shoulder of the hill I looked eagerly for the first glimpse of the barn. I confess that I had woven a thousand stories to explain the mystery, and had reached the point where I could no longer resist seeing if I could solve it.

Well, the barn was transformed. Two or three new windows, a door with a little porch, a lattice or so for vines, a gable upon the roof lifting an inquiring eye-brow--and what was once a barn had become a charming cottage. It seemed curiously to have come alive, to have acquired a personality of its own. A corner of the great garden had been cut off and included in the miniature grounds of the cottage; and a simple arbour had been built against a background of wonderful beech trees. You felt at once a kind of fondness for it.

I saw Mary Starkweather in her garden, in a large straw hat, with a trowel in her hand.

"How are you, David Grayson?" she called out when I stopped.

"I have been planning for several days," I said, "to happen casually by your new house."

"Have you?"

"You don't know how you have stirred our curiosity. We haven't had a good night's rest since you moved in."

"I've no doubt of it," she laughed. "Won't you come in? I'd like to tell you all about it."

"I also prepared to make excuses for not stopping," I said, "and thought up various kinds of urgent business, such as buying a new snow shovel to use next winter, but after making these excuses I intended to stop--if I were sufficiently urged."

"You are more than urged: you are commanded."

As I followed her up the walk she said earnestly:

"Will you do me a favour? When you come in will you tell me the first impression my living-room gives you? No second thoughts. Tell me instantly."

"I'll do it." I said, my mind leaping eagerly to all manner of mysterious surprises.

At the centre of the room she turned toward me and with a sweeping backward motion of the arms, made me a bow--a strong figure instinct with confident grace: a touch of gray in the hair, a fleeting look of old sadness about the eyes.

"Now, David Grayson," she said, "quick!"

It was not that the room itself was so remarkable as that it struck me as being confusingly different from the heavily comfortable rooms of the old Starkweather house with their crowded furnishings, their overloaded mantels, their plethoric bookcases.

"I cannot think of you yet," I stumbled, "as being here."

"Isn't it *like* me?"

"It is a beautiful room--" I groped lamely.

"I was afraid you would say that."

"But it is. It really is."

"Then I've failed, after all."

She said it lightly enough, but there was an undertone of real disappointment in her voice.

"I'm in rather the predicament," I said, "of old Abner Coates. You probably don't know Abner. He sells nursery stock, and each spring when he comes around and I tell him that the peach trees or the raspberry bushes I bought of him the year before have not done well, he says, with the greatest astonishment, 'Wal, now, ye ain't said what I hoped ye would.' I see that I haven't said what you hoped I would."

It was too serious a matter, however, for Mary Starkweather to joke about.

"But, David Grayson," she said, "isn't it *simple*?"

I glanced around me with swift new comprehension.

"Why, yes, it *is* simple."

I saw that my friend was undergoing some deep inner change of which this room, this renovated barn, were mere symbols.

"Tell me," I said, "how you came to such a right-about-face."

"It's just that!" she returned earnestly, "It *is* a right-about-face. I think I am really in earnest for the first time in my life."

I had a moment of flashing wonder if her marriage had not been in earnest, a flashing picture of Richard Starkweather with his rather tired, good-humoured face, and I wondered if her children were not earnest realities to her, if her busy social life had meant nothing. Then I reflected that we all have such moments, when the richest experiences of the past seem as nothing in comparison with the fervour of this glowing moment.

"Everything in my life in the past," she was saying, "seems to have happened to me. Life has done things *for* me; I have had so few chances of doing anything for myself."

"And now you are expressing yourself."

"Almost for the first time in my life!"

She paused. "All my life, it seems to me, I have been smothered with things. Just things! Too much of everything. All my time has been taken up in caring for things and none in enjoying them."

"I understand!" I said with a warm sense of corroboration and sympathy.

"I had so many pictures on my walls that I never saw, really saw, any of them. I saw the dust on them, I saw the cracks in the frames, that needed repairing, I even saw better ways of arranging them, but I very rarely saw, with the inner eye, what the artists were trying to tell me. And how much time I have wasted on mere food and clothing--it is appalling! I had become nothing short of a slave to my house and my things."

"I see now," I said, "why you have just one rose on your table."

"Yes"--she returned eagerly--"isn't it a beauty! I spent half an hour this morning looking for the best and most perfect rose in the garden, and there it is!"

She was now all alight with her idea, and I saw her, as we sometimes see our oldest friends, as though I had not seen her before. She was that phenomenon of the modern world--the free woman of forty-five.

When a woman reaches the old age of youth, the years between forty and forty-five, she either surrenders or revolts. In the older days in America it was nearly always surrender. Those women of a past generation bore many children: how many graves there are in our hill cemeteries of women of forty to fifty who died leading families of five or eight or ten children! How many second and third wives there were, often with second and third families. Or if they did not die, how terribly they toiled, keeping the house, clothing the children, cooking the food. Or if they bore no children, yet they were bound down by a thousand chains of convention and formality.

But in these days we have a woman of forty-five who has not surrendered. She is a vigorous, experienced, active-minded human being, just beginning to look restlessly around her and take a new interest in the world. Such a woman was Mary Starkweather; and this was her first revolt.

"You cannot imagine," she was saying, "what a joy it has been to unaccumulate! To get rid of things! To select."

"To become an artist in life!"

"Yes! At last! What a lot of perfectly worthless trash accumulates around us.

Not beautiful, not even useful! And it is not only the lives of the well-to-do that are choked and cluttered with things. I wish you could see the house of our Polish farmer. He's been saving money, and filling up his house with perfectly worthless ornaments--ornate clocks, gorgeous plush furniture, impossible rugs--and yet he is only doing what we are all doing on a more elaborate scale."

I laughed.

"That reminds me of a family of squirrels that lives in an oak tree on my hill," I said. "I am never tired of watching them. In the fall they work desperately, stealing all the hickory nuts and chestnuts on my neighbour Horace's back pastures, five times as many as they need, and then they forget, half the time, where they've hidden them. We're all more or less in the squirrel stage of civilization."

"Yes," she responded. "There are my books! I gathered up books for years, just squirrel fashion, until I forgot what I had or where I put them. You cannot know what joy I'm going to have in selecting just the essential books, the ones I want by me for daily companions. All the others, I see now, are temporary rubbish."

"And you've made your selections?"

"No, but I'm making them. You'll laugh when you come next time and I show them to you. Oh, I am going to be stern with myself. I'm not going to put a single book in that case for show, nor a single one to give the impression that I'm profoundly interested in Egypt or Maeterlinck or woman suffrage, when I'm positively not."

"It's terribly risky," I said.

"And I'm terribly reckless," she responded.

As I went onward toward the town I looked back from the hilltop beyond the big house for a last glimpse of the reconstructed barn, and with a curious warm sense of having been admitted to a new adventure. Here was life changing under my eyes! Here was a human being struggling with one of the deep common problems that come to all of us. The revolt from things! The struggle with superfluities!

And yet as I walked along the cool aisles of the woods with the quiet fields opening here and there to the low hill ridges, and saw the cattle feeding, and heard a thrush singing in a thicket, I found myself letting go--how can I explain it?-- relaxing! I had been keyed up to a high pitch there in that extraordinary room, Yes, it ***was*** beautiful--and yet as I thought of the sharp little green gate, the new gable, the hard, clean mantel with the cloisonne vase, it wanted something....

As I was gathering the rowen crop of after-enjoyment which rewards us when we reflect freshly upon our adventures, whom should I meet but Richard Starkweather himself in his battered machine. The two boys, one of whom was driving, and the little girl, were with him.

"How are you, David?" he called out. "Whoa, there! Draw up, Jamie."

We looked at each other for a moment with that quizzical, half-humorous look that so often conveys, better than any spoken words, the sympathetic greeting of friends. I like Richard Starkweather.

He had come up from the city looking rather worn, for the weather had been trying. He has blue, honest, direct-gazing eyes with small humour wrinkles at the corners. I never knew a man with fewer theories, or with a simpler devotion to the thing at hand, whatever it may be. At everything else he smiles, not cynically, for he is too modest in his regard for his own knowledge; he smiles at everything else because it doesn't seem quite real to him.

"Been up to see Mary's new house?" he asked.

"Yes," And for the life of me I couldn't help smiling in response.

"It's a wonder isn't it?"

He thought his wife a very extraordinary woman. I remember his saying to me once, "David, she's got the soul of a poet and the brain of a general."

"It *is* a wonder," I responded.

"I can't decide yet what chair to sit in, nor just what she wants the kids to do."

I still smiled.

"I expect she hasn't determined yet," he went drawling on, "in what chair I will look most decorative."

He ruminated.

"You know, she's got the idea that there's too much of everything. I guess there is, too--and that she ought to select only those things that an essential. I've been wondering, if she had more than one husband whether or not she'd select me----"

The restless young Jamie was now starting the machine, and Richard Starkweather leaned out and said to me in parting: "isn't she a wonder! Did all the planning herself--wouldn't have an architect--wouldn't have a decorator--all I could do--"

As he turned around I saw him throw one arm carelessly about the shoulders of the sturdy younger boy who sat next him.

When I got home I told Harriet all about what I had seen and heard. I think I must feel when I am retailing such fascinating neighbourhood events to Harriet-- how she *does* enjoy them!--I must feel very much as she does when she is urging me to have just a little more of the new gingerbread.

In the next few months I watched with indescribable interest the unfolding of the drama of Mary Starkweather. I saw her from time to time that summer and she seemed, and I think she was, happier than ever she had been before in her whole life. Making over her garden, selecting the "essential books," choosing the best pictures for her rooms, even reforming the clothing of the boys, all with an emphasis upon perfect simplicity--her mind was completely absorbed. Occasionally Richard appeared upon the stage, a kind of absurd Greek chorus of one, who remarked what a wonderful woman this was and poked fun at himself and at the new house, and asserted that Mary could be as simple as ever she liked, he insisted on thick soup for dinner and would not sacrifice his beloved old smoking jacket upon the altar of any new idea.

"She's a wonder, David," he'd wind up: "but this simple life is getting more complicated every day."

It was in December, about the middle of the month, as I remember, that I had a note one day from Mary Starkweather.

"The next time you go to town," it ran, "stop in and see me. I've made a discovery."

With such a note as that us my hand it appeared imperative that I go to town at once. I discovered, to Harriet's astonishment, that we were running out of all sorts of necessaries.

"Now, David," she said, "you know perfectly well that you're just making up to call on Mary Starkweather."

"That," I said, "relieves my conscience of a great burden."

As I went out of the door I heard her saying: "Why Mary Starkweather should *care* to live in her barn...."

It was a sparkling cold day, sun on the snow and the track crunching under one's feet, and I walked swiftly and with a warm sense of coming adventure.

To my surprise there was no smoke in the cottage chimney, and when I reached the door I found a card pinned upon it:

PLEASE CALL AT THE HOUSE

Mary Starkweather herself opened the door--she had seen me coming--and took me into the big comfortable old living-room, the big, cluttered, overfurnished living-room, with the two worn upholstered chairs at the fireplace, in which a bright log fire was now burning. There was a pleasant litter of books and magazines, and a work basket on the table, and in the bay window an ugly but cheerful green rubber plant in a tub.

"Well!" I exclaimed.

"Don't smile--not yet."

As I looked at her I felt not at all like smiling.

"I know," she was saying, "it does have a humorous side. I can see that. Dick has seen it all along. Do you know, although Dick pretends to pooh-pooh everything intellectual, he has a really penetrating mind."

I had a sudden vision of Dick in his old smoking jacket, standing in the midst of the immaculate cottage that was once a barn, holding his pipe with one finger crooked around the stem just in front of his nose in the way he had, and smiling across at me.

"Have you deserted the cottage entirely?"

"Oh, we may possibly go back in the spring-----" She paused and looked into the fire, her fine, strong face a little sad in composure, full of thought.

"I am trying to be honest with myself David. Honest above everything else. That's fundamental. It seems to me I have wanted most of all to learn how to live my life more freely and finely.... I thought I was getting myself free of things when, as a matter of fact, I was devoting more time to them than ever before-and, besides that, making life more or less uncomfortable for Dick and the children. So I've taken my courage squarely in my hands and come back here into this blessed old home, this blessed, ugly, stuffy old home--I've learned *that* lesson."

At this, she glanced up at me with that rare smile which sometimes shines out of her very nature: the smile that is herself.

"I found," she said, "that when I had finished the work of becoming simple-- there was nothing else left to do."

I laughed outright, for I couldn't help it, and she joined me. How we do like people who can laugh at themselves.

"But," I said, "there was sound sense in a great deal that you were trying to do."

"The fireplace smoked; and the kitchen sink froze up; and the cook left because we couldn't keep her room warm."

"But you were right," I interrupted, "and I am not going to be put off by smoking fireplaces or chilly cooks; you were right. We do have too much, we are smothered in things, we don't enjoy what we do have--"

I paused.

"And you were making a beautiful thing, a beautiful house."

"The trouble with making a beautiful thing," she replied, "is that when you have got it done you must straightway make another. Now I don't want to keep on building houses or furnishing rooms. I am not after beauty--I mean primarily--what I want is to **live**, live simply, live greatly."

She was desperately in earnest.

"Perhaps," I said, feeling as though I were treading on dangerous ground, "you were trying to be simple for the sake of being simple. I wonder if true simplicity is ever any thing but a by-product. If we aim directly for it, it eludes us: but if we are on fire with some great interest that absorbs on lives to the uttermost, we forget ourselves into simplicity, Everything falls into simple lines around us, like a worn garment."

I had the rather uncomfortable feeling on the way home that I had been preachy; and the moment you became preachy begin to build up barriers between yourself and your friends: but that's a defect of character I've never been able, quite, to overcome. I keep thinking I've got the better of it, but along will come a beautiful temptation and down I go--and come out as remorseful as I was that afternoon on the way home from Mary Starkweather's.

A week or two later I happened to meet Richard Starkweather on the street in Hempfield. He was on his way home. "Yes," he said, "we're in the old house again until spring, anyway. I haven't been so comfortable in a year. And, say," here he looked at me quizzically, "Mary has joined the new cemetery association; you know they're trying to improve the resting places of the forefathers, and, by George, if they didn't elect her chairman at the first meeting. She's a wonder!"

CHAPTER XIII
HIS MAJESTY--BILL RICHARDS

Well, I have just been having an amusing and delightful adventure and have come to know a Great Common Person. His name is Bill Richards, and he is one of the hereditary monarchs of America. He belongs to our ruling dynasty.

I first saw Bill about two weeks ago, and while I was strongly interested in him I had no idea, at the time, that I should ever come to know him well. It was a fine June day, and I was riding on the new trolley line that crosses the hills to Hewlett--a charming trip through a charming country--and there in the open car just in front of me sat Bill himself. One huge bare forearm rested on the back of the seat, the rich red blood showing through the weathered brown of the skin. His clean brown neck rose strongly from the loose collar of his shirt, which covered but could not hide the powerful lines of his shoulders. He wore blue denim and khaki, and a small round felt hat tipped up jauntily at the back. He had crisp, coarse light hair rather thin--not by age, but by nature--so that the ruddy scalp could be seen through it, and strong jaws and large firm features, and if the beard was two days old, his face was so brown, so full of youthful health, that it gave no ill impression.

He could not sit still for the very life that was in him. He seemed to have some grand secret with the conductor and frequently looked around at him, his eyes full of careless laughter, and once or twice he called out--some jocose remark. He helped the conductor, in pantomime, to pull the cord and stop or start the car, and he watched with the liveliest interest each passenger getting on or getting off. A rather mincing young girl with a flaring red ribbon at her throat was to him the finest comedy in the world, so that he had to wink a telegram to the conductor about her. An old woman with a basket of vegetables who delayed the car was exquisitely funny.

I set him down as being about twenty-two years old and some kind of outdoor workman, not a farmer.

When he got off, which was before the car stopped, so that he had to jump and run with it, he gave a wild flourish with both arms, grimaced at the conductor, and went off down the road whistling for all he was worth. How I enjoyed the sight of him! He was so charged with youthful energy, so overflowing with the joy of life, that he could scarcely contain himself. What a fine place the world was to him! And what comical and interesting people it contained! I was sorry when he got off.

Two or three days later I was on my way up the town road north of my farm when I was astonished and delighted to see Bill for the second time. He was coming down the road pulling a wire over the crosspiece of a tall telephone pole (the company is rebuilding and enlarging its system through our town). He was holding the wire close drawn over his right shoulder, his strong hands gripped and pressed upon his breast. The veins stood out in his brown neck where the burlap shoulder pad he wore was drawn aside by the wire. He leaned forward, stepping first on his toe, which he dug into the earth and then, heavily letting down his heel, he drew the other foot forward somewhat stiffly. The muscles stood out in his powerful shoulders and thighs. His legs were double-strapped with climbing spurs. He was a master lineman.

As I came alongside he turned a good-humoured sweaty face toward me.

"It's dang hot," said he.

"It is," said I.

There is something indescribably fascinating about the sight of a strong workman in the full swing of his work, something--yes, beautiful! A hard pull of a job, with a strong man doing it joyfully, what could be finer to see? And he gave such a jaunty sense of youth and easy strength!

I watched him for some time, curiously interested, and thought I should like well to know him, but could not see just how to go about it.

The man astride the cross-arm who was heaving the wire forward from the spool on the distant truck suddenly cried out:

"Ease up there, Bill, she's caught."

So Bill eased up and drew his arm across his dripping face.

"How many wires are you putting up?" I asked, fencing for some opening.

"Three," said Bill.

Before I could get in another stroke the man on the pole shouted:

"Let 'er go, Bill." And Bill let 'er go, and buckled down again to his job.

"Gee, but it's hot," said he.

In the country there are not so many people passing our way that we cannot be interested in all of them. That evening I could not help thinking about Bill, the lineman, wondering where he came from, how he happened to be what he was, who and what sort were the friends he made, and the nature of his ambitions, if he had any. Talk about going to the North Pole! It is not to be compared, for downright fascination, with the exploration of an undiscovered human being.

With that I began to think how I might get at Bill, the lineman, and not merely weather talk, or wages talk, or work talk, but at Bill himself. He was a character quite unusual in our daily lives here in the country. I wondered what his interests could be, surely not mine nor Horace's nor the Starkweathers'. As soon as I began trying to visualize what his life might be, I warmed up to a grand scheme of capturing him, if by chance he was to be found the next day upon the town road.

All this may seem rather absurd in the telling, but I found it a downright good adventure for a quiet evening, and fully believe I felt for the moment like General Joffre planning to meet the Germans on the Marne.

"I have it!" I said aloud.

"You have what?" asked Harriet, somewhat startled.

"The grandest piece of strategy ever devised in this town," said I.

With that I went delving in a volume of universal information I keep near me, one of those knowing books that tells you how tall the great Pryamid is and why a hen cackles after laying an egg, and having found what I wanted I asked Harriet if she could find a tape measure around the place. She is a wonderful person and knows where everything is. When she handed me the tape measure she asked me what in the world I was so mysterious about.

"Harriet," I said, "I'm going on a great adventure. I'll tell you all about it to-morrow."

"Nonsense," said Harriet.

It is this way with the fancies of the evening--they often look flat and flabby and gray the next morning. Quite impossible! But if I'd acted on half the good and grand schemes I've had o' nights I might now be quite a remarkable person.

I went about my work the next morning just as usual. I even avoided looking at the little roll of tape on the corner of the mantel as I went out. It seemed a kind of badge of my absurdity. But about the middle of the fore-noon, while I was in my garden, I heard a tremendous racket up the road. Rattle--bang, zip, toot! As I looked up I saw the boss lineman and his crew careering up the road in their truck, and the bold driver was driving like Jehu, the son of Nimshi. And there were ladders and poles clattering out behind, and rolls of wire on upright spools rattling and flashing in the sunshine, and the men of the crew were sitting along the sides of the truck with hats off and hair flying as they came bumping and bounding up the road. It was a brave thing to see going by on a spring morning!

As they passed, whom should I see but Bill himself, at the top of the load, with a broad smile on his face. When his eye fell on me he threw up one arm, and gave me the railroad salute.

"Hey, there!" he shouted.

"Hey there, yourself," I shouted in return--and could not help it.

I had a curious warm feeling of being taken along with that jolly crowd of workmen, with Bill on the top of the load.

It was this that finished me. I hurried through an early dinner, and taking the tape measure off the mantel I put it in my pocket as though it were a revolver or a bomb, and went off up the road feeling as adventurous as ever I felt in my life. I never said a word to Harriet but disappeared quietly around the lilac bushes. I was going to waylay that crew, and especially Bill. I hoped to catch them at their noon-ing.

Well, I was lucky. About a quarter of a mile up the road, in a little valley near the far corner of Horace's farm, I found the truck, and Bill just getting out his dinner pail. It seems they had flipped pennies and Bill hod been left behind with the truck and the tools while the others went down to the mill pond in the valley below.

"How are you?" said I.

"How are *you*?" said he.

I could see that he was rather cross over having been left behind.

"Fine day," said I.

"You bet," said he.

He got out his pail, which was a big one, and seated himself on the roadside, a grassy, comfortable spot near the brook which runs below into the pond. There were white birches and hemlocks on the hill, and somewhere in the thicket I heard a wood thrush singing.

"Did you ever see John L. Sullivan?" I asked.

He glanced up at me quickly, but with new interest.

"No, did you?"

"Or Bob Fitzsimmons?"

"Nope--but I was mighty near it once. I've seen 'em both in the movies."

"Well, sir," said I, "that's interesting. I should like to see them myself. Do you know what made me speak of them?"

He had spread down a newspaper and was taking the luncheon out of his "bucket," as he called it, including a large bottle of coffee; but he paused and looked at me with keen interest.

"Well," said I, "when I saw you dragging that wire yesterday I took you to be a pretty husky citizen yourself."

He grinned and took a big mouthful from one of his sandwiches. I could see that my shot had gone home.

"So when I got back last night," I said, "I looked up the arm measurements of Sullivan and Fitzsimmons in a book I have and got to wondering how they compared with mine and yours. They were considerably larger than mine--"

Bill thought this a fine joke and laughed out in great good humour.

"But I imagine you'd not be far behind either of them."

He looked at me a little suspiciously, as if doubtful what I was driving at or whether or not I was joking him. But I was as serious as the face of nature; and proceeded at once to get out my tape measure.

"I get very much interested in such things," I said, "and I had enough curiosity to want to see how big your arm really was."

He smiled broadly.

"You're a queer one," said he.

But he took another bite of sandwich, and clenching his great fist drew up his forearm until the biceps muscles looked like a roll of Vienna bread--except that they had the velvety gleam of life. So I measured first one arm, then the other.

"By George!" said I, "you're ahead of Fitzsimmons, but not quite up to Sullivan."

"Fitz wasn't a heavy man," said Bill, "but a dead game fighter."

I saw then that I had him! So I sat down on the grass near by and we had great talk about the comparative merits of Fitzsimmons and Sullivan and Corbett and Jack Johnson, a department of knowledge in which he out-distanced me. He even told me of an exploit or two of his own, which showed that he was able to take care of himself.

While we talked he ate his luncheon, and a downright gargantuan luncheon it was, backed by an appetite which if it were offered to the highest bidder on the New York Stock Exchange would, I am convinced, bring at least ten thousand dollars in cash. It even made me envious.

There were three huge corned-beef sandwiches, three hard-boiled eggs, a pickle six inches long and fat to boot, four doughnuts so big that they resembled pitching quoits, a bottle of coffee and milk, a quarter of a pie, and, to cap the climax, an immense raw onion. It was worth a long journey to see Bill eat that onion. He took out his clasp knife, and after stripping off the papery outer shell, cut the onion into thick dewy slices. Then he opened one of the sandwiches and placed several of them on the beef, afterward sprinkling them with salt from a small paper parcel. Having restored the top slice of bread he took a moon-shaped bite out of one end of this glorified sandwich.

"I like onions," said he.

When we first sat down he had offered to share his luncheon with me but I told him I had just been to dinner, and I observed that he had no difficulty in taking care of every crumb in his "bucket." It was wonderful to see.

Having finished his luncheon he went down to the brook and got a drink, and then sat down comfortably with his back among the ferns of the roadside, crossed his legs, and lit his pipe. There was a healthy and wholesome flush in his face, and as he blew off the first cloud of smoke he drew a sigh of complete comfort and looked around at me with a lordly air such as few monarchs, no matter how well fed, could have bettered. He had worked and sweat for what he got, and was now taking his ease in his roadside inn. I wonder sometimes if anybody in the world experiences keener joys than unwatched common people.

How we talked! From pugilists we proceeded to telephones, and from that to wages, hours, and strikes, and from that we leaped easily to Alaska and gold-mining, and touched in passing upon Theodore Roosevelt.

"I was just thinking," I said, "that you and I can enjoy some things that were beyond the reach of the greatest kings of the world."

"How's that?" said he.

"Why, Napoleon never saw a telephone nor talked through one."

"That's so!" he laughed.

"And Caesar couldn't have dreamed that such a thing as you are doing now was a possibility--nor George Washington, either."

"Say, that's so. I never thought o' that."

"Why," I said, "the world is only half as big as it was before you fellows came along stringing your wires! I can get to town now from my farm in two minutes, when it used to take me an hour."

I really believe I gave him more of his own business than ever he had before, for he listened so intently that his pipe went out.

I found that Bill was from Ohio, and that he had been as far south as Atlanta and as far west as Denver. He got his three dollars and a half a day, rain or shine, and thought it wonderful pay; and besides, he was seein' the country "free, gratis, fer nothing."

He got his coat out of the truck and took from the pocket a many-coloured folder.

"Say, Mister, have you ever been to the Northwest?"

"No," said I.

"Well, it's a great country, and I'm goin' up there."

He spread out the glittering folder and placed his big forefinger on a spot about the size of Rhode Island somewhere this side of the Rockies.

"How'll you do it?" I asked.

"Oh, a lineman can go anywhere," said he with a flourish, "A lineman don't have to beg a job. Besides, I got eighty dollars sewed up."

Talk about freedom! Never have I got a clearer impression of it than Bill gave me that day. No millionaire, no potentate, could touch him.

The crew came back all too soon for me. Bill knocked the ashes out of his pipe on his boot heel, and put his "bucket" back in the truck. Five minutes later he was climbing a tall pole with legs bowed out, striking in his spikes at each step. From the cross-arm, up among the hemlock tops, he called out to me:

"Good-bye, pard."

"Stop in, Bill, and see me when you come by my place," said I.

"You bet," said he.

And he did, the next day, and I showed him off to Harriet, who brought him a plate of her best doughnuts and asked him about his mother.

Yesterday I saw him again careering by in the truck. The job was finished. He waved his hand at me.

"I'm off," said he.

"Where?" I shouted.

"Canada."

CHAPTER XIV
ON LIVING IN THE COUNTRY

"Why risk with men your hard won gold*?
Buy grain and sow your Brother Dust
Will pay you back a hundred fold--
The earth commits no breach of trust."

Hindu Proverb, Translated by Arthur Guiterman.

I t is astonishing how many people there are in cities and towns who have a secret longing to get back into quiet country places, to own a bit of the soil of the earth, and to cultivate it. To some it appears as a troublesome malady only in spring and will be relieved by a whirl or two in country roads, by a glimpse of the hills, or a day by the sea; but to others the homesickness is deeper seated and will be quieted by no hasty visits. These must actually go home.

I have had, in recent years, many letters from friends asking about life in the country, but the longer I remain here, the more I know about it, the less able I am to answer them--at least briefly. It is as though one should come and ask: "Is love worth trying?" or, "How about religion?" For country life is to each human being a fresh, strange, original adventure. We enjoy it, or we do not enjoy it, or more probably, we do both. It is packed and crowded with the zest of adventure, or it is dull and miserable. We may, if we are skilled enough, make our whole living from the land, or only a part of it, or we may find in a few cherished acres the inspiration and power for other work, whatever it may be. There is many a man whose strength is renewed like that of the wrestler of Irassa, every time his feet touch the earth.

Of all places in the world where life can be lived to its fullest and freest, where it can be met in its greatest variety and beauty, I am convinced that there is none to equal the open country, or the country town. For all country people in these days may have the city--some city or town not too far away: but there are millions of men and women in America who have no country and no sense of the country. What do they not lose out of life!

I know well the disadvantages charged against country life at its worst. At its worst there are long hours and much lonely labour and an income pitifully small. Drudgery, yes, especially for the women, and loneliness. But where is there not drudgery when men are poor--where life is at its worst? I have never seen drudgery in the country comparable for a moment to the dreary and lonely drudgery of city tenements, city mills, factories, and sweat shops. And in recent years both the drudgery and loneliness of country life have been disappearing before the motor and trolley car, the telephone, the rural post, the gasoline engine. I have seen a machine plant as many potatoes in one day as a man, at hand work, could have planted in a week. While there is, indeed, real drudgery in the country, much that is looked upon as drudgery by people who long for easy ways and a soft life, is only good, honest, wholesome hard work--the kind of work that makes for fiber in a man or in a nation, the kind that most city life in no wise provides.

There are a thousand nuisances and annoyances that men must meet who come face to face with nature itself. You have set out your upper acres to peach trees: and the deer come down from the hills at night and strip the young foliage; or the field mice in winter, working under the snow, girdle and kill them. The season brings too much rain and the potatoes rot in the ground, the crows steal the corn, the bees swarm when no out is watching, the cow smothers her calf, the hens' eggs prove infertile, and a storm in a day ravages a crop that has been growing all summer. A constant warfare with insects and blights and fungi--a real, bitter warfare, which can cease neither summer nor winter!

It is something to meet, year after year, the quiet implacability of the land. While it is patient, it never waits long for you. There is a chosen time for planting, a time for cultivating, a time for harvesting. You accept the gauge thrown down-- well and good, you shall have a chance to fight! You do not accept it? There is no complaint. The land cheerfully springs up to wild yellow mustard and dandelion and pig-weed--and will be productive and beautiful in spite of you.

Nor can you enter upon the full satisfaction of cultivating even a small piece of land at second hand. To be accepted as One Who Belongs, there must be sweat and weariness.

The other day I was digging with Dick in a ditch that is to run down through the orchard and connect finally with the land drain we put in four years ago. We laid the tile just in the gravel below the silt, about two feet deep, covering the openings with tar paper and then throwing in gravel. It was a bright, cool afternoon. In the field below a ploughman was at work: I could see the furrows of the dark earth glisten as he turned it over. The grass in the meadow was a full rich green, the new chickens were active in their yards, running to the cluck of the hens, already the leaves of the orchard trees showed green. And as I worked there with Dick I had the curious deep feeling of coming somehow into a new and more intimate possession of my own land. For titles do not really pass with signatures and red seals, nor with money changing from one hand to another, but for true possession one must work and serve according to the most ancient law. There is no mitigation and no haggling of price. Those who think they can win the greatest joys of country life on any easier terms are mistaken.

But if one has drained his land, and ploughed it, and fertilized it, and planted it and harvested it--even though it be only a few acres-- how he comes to know and to love every rod of it. He knows the wet spots, and the stony spots, and the warmest and most fertile spots --until his acres have all the qualities of a personality, whose every characteristic he knows. It is so also that he comes to know his horses and cattle and pigs and hens. It is a fine thing, on a warm day in early spring, to bring out the bee-hives and let the bees have their first flight in the sunshine. What cleanly folk they are! And later to see them coming in yellow all over with pollen from the willows! It is a fine thing to watch the cherries and plum trees come into blossom, with us about the first of May, while all the remainder of the orchard seems still sleeping. It is a fine thing to see the cattle turned for the first time in spring into the green meadows. It is a fine thing--one of the finest of all--to see and smell the rain in a corn-field after weeks of drought. How it comes softly out of gray skies, the first drops throwing up spatters of dust and losing themselves in the dry soil. Then the clouds sweep forward up the valley, darkening the meadows and blotting out the hills, and then there is the whispering of the rain as it first sweeps across the corn-field. At once what a stir of life! What rustling of the long green leaves. What joyful shaking and swaying of the tassels! And have you watched how eagerly the grooved leaves catch the early drops, and, lest there be too little rain after all, conduct them jealously down the stalks where they will soonest reach the thirsty roots? What a fine thing is this to see!

One who thus takes part in the whole process of the year comes soon to have an indescribable affection for his land, his garden, his animals. There are thoughts of his in every tree: memories in every fence corner. Just now, the fourth of June, I walked down past my blackberry patch, now come gorgeously into full white bloom--and heavy with fragrance. I set out these plants with my own hands, I have fed them, cultivated them, mulched them, pruned them, trellised them, and helped every year to pick the berries. How could they be otherwise than full of as-sociations! They bear a fruit more beautiful than can be found in any catalogue: and stranger and wilder than in any learned botany book!

Why, one who comes thus to love a bit of countryside may enjoy it all the year round. When he awakens in the middle of a long winter night he may send his mind out to the snowy fields--I've done it a thousand times!--and visit each part in turn, stroll through the orchard and pay his respects to each tree--in a small or-chard one comes to know familiarly every tree as he knows his friends--stop at the strawberry bed, consider the grape trellises, feel himself opening the door of the warm, dark stable and listening to the welcoming whicker of his horses, or visiting his cows, his pigs, his sheep, his hens, or so many of them as he may have.

So much of the best in the world seems to have come fragrant out of fields, gar-dens, and hillsides. So many truths spoken by the Master Poet come to us exhaling the odours of the open country. His stories were so often of sowers, husbandmen, herdsmen: his similes and illustrations so often dealt with the common and familiar beauty of the fields. "Consider the lilies how they grow." It was on a hillside that he preached his greatest Sermon, and when in the last agony he sought a place to meet his God, where did he go but to a garden? A carpenter you say? Yes, but of this one may be sure: there were gardens and fields all about: he knew gardens, and cattle, and the simple processes of the land: he must have worked in a garden and loved it well.

A country life rather spoils one for the so-called luxuries. A farmer or gardener may indeed have a small cash income, but at least he eats at the first table. He may have the sweetest of the milk, there are thousands, perhaps millions, of men and women in America who have never in their lives tasted really sweet milk and the freshest of eggs, and the ripest of fruit. One does not know how good strawberries or raspberries are when picked before breakfast and eaten with the dew still on them. And while he must work and sweat for what he gets, he may have all these things in almost unmeasured abundance, and without a thought of what they cost. A man from the country is often made uncomfortable, upon visiting the city, to find two cans of sweet corn served for twenty or thirty cents, or a dish of raspberries at twenty-five or forty--and neither, even at their best, equal in quality to those he may have fresh from the garden every day. One need say this in no boastful spirit, but as a simple statement of the fact: for fruits sent to the city are nearly always picked before they are fully ripe--and lose that last perfection of flavour which the sun and the open air impart: and both fruits and vegetables, as well as milk and eggs, suffer more than most people think from handling and shipment. These things can be set down as one of the make-weights against the familiar presentation of the farmer's life as a hard one.

One of the greatest curses of mill or factory work and with much city work of all kinds, is its interminable monotony: the same process repeated hour after hour and day after day. In the country there is indeed monotonous work but rarely monotony. No task continues very long: everything changes infinitely with the seasons. Processes are not repetitive but creative. Nature hates monotony, is ever changing and restless, brings up a storm to drive the haymakers from their hurried work in the fields, sends rain to stop the ploughing, or a frost to hurry the apple harvest. Everything is full of adventure and vicissitude! A man who has been a farmer for two hours at the mowing must suddenly turn blacksmith when his machine breaks down and tinker with wrench and hammer; and later in the day he becomes dairyman, farrier, harness-maker, merchant. No kind of wheat but is grist to his mill, no knowledge that he cannot use! And who is freer to be a citizen than he: freer to take his part in town meeting and serve his state in some one of the innumerable small offices which form the solid blocks of organization beneath our commonwealth.

I thought last fall that corn-husking came as near being monotonous work, as any I had ever done in the country. I presume in the great corn-fields of the West, where the husking goes on for weeks at a time, it probably does grow really monotonous. But I soon found that there was a curious counter-reward attending even a process as repetitive as this.

I remember one afternoon in particular. It was brisk and cool with ragged clouds like flung pennants in a poverty-stricken sky, and the hills were a hazy brown, rather sad to see, and in one of the apple trees at the edge of the meadow the crows were holding their mournful autumn parliament.

At such work as this one's mind often drops asleep, or at least goes dreaming, except for the narrow margin of awareness required for the simple processes of the hands. Its orders have indeed been given: you must kneel here, pull aside the stalks one by one, rip down the husks, and twist off the ear--and there is the pile for the stripped stalks, and here the basket for the gathered corn, and these processes infinitely repeated.

While all this is going on, the mind itself wanders off to its own far sweet pastures, upon its own dear adventures--or rests, or plays. It is in these times that most of the airy flying things of this beautiful world come home to us--things that heavy-footed reason never quite overtakes, nor stodgy knowledge ever knows. I think sometimes (as Sterne says) we thus intercept thoughts never intended for us at all, or uncover strange primitive memories of older times than these--racial memories.

At any rate, the hours pass and suddenly the mind comes home again, it comes home from its wanderings refreshed, stimulated, happy. And nowhere, whether in cities, or travelling in trains, or sailing upon the sea, have I so often felt this curious enrichment as I have upon this hillside, working alone in field, or garden, or orchard, It seems to come up out of the soil, or respond to the touch of growing things.

What makes any work interesting is the fact that one can make experiments, try new things, develop specialties and *grow*. And where can he do this with such success as on the land and in direct contact with nature. The possibilities are here infinite new machinery, spraying, seed testing, fertilizers, experimentation with new varieties. A thousand and one methods, all creative, which may be tried out in that great essential struggle of the farmer or gardener to command all the forces of nature.

Because there are farmers, and many of them, who do not experiment and do

not grow, but make their occupation a veritable black drudgery, this is no reason
for painting a sombre-hued picture of country life. Any calling, the law, the minis-
try, the medical profession, can be blasted by fixing one's eyes only upon its ugliest
aspects. And farming, at its best, has become a highly scientific, extraordinarily
absorbing, and when all is said, a profitable, profession. Neighbours of mine have
developed systems of overhead irrigation to make rain when there is no rain, and
have covered whole fields with cloth canopies to increase the warmth and to pro-
tect the crops from wind and hail, and by the analysis of the soil and exact methods
of feeding it with fertilizers, have come as near a complete command of nature as
any farmers in the world. What independent, resourceful men they are! And many
of them have also grown rich in money. It is not what nature does with a man that
matters but what he does with nature.

Nor is it necessary in these days for the farmer or the country dweller to be
uncultivated or uninterested in what are often called, with no very clear definition,
the "finer things of life." Many educated men are now on the farms and have their
books and magazines, and their music and lectures and dramas not too far off in
the towns. A great change in this respect has come over American country life in
twenty years. The real hardships of pioneering have passed away, and with good
roads and machinery, and telephones, and newspapers every day by rural post, the
farmer may maintain as close a touch with the best things the world has to offer as
any man. And if he really have such broader interests the winter furnishes him time
and leisure that no other class of people can command.

I do not know, truly, what we are here for upon this wonderful and beautiful earth, this incalculably interesting earth, unless it is to crowd into a few short
years--when all is said, terribly short years!--every possible fine experience and adventure: unless it is to live our lives to the uttermost: unless it is to seize upon every
fresh impression, develop every latent capacity: to grow as much as ever we have it
in our power to grow. What else can there be? If there is no life beyond this one, we
have lived *here* to the uttermost. We've had what we've had! But if there is more
life, and still more life, beyond this one, and above and under this one, and around
and through this one, we shall be well prepared for that, whatever it may be.

The real advantages of country life have come to be a strong lure to many
people in towns and cities: but no one should attempt to "go back to the land" with

the idea that it is an easy way to escape the real problems and difficulties of life. The fact is, there is no escape. The problems and the difficulties must be boldly met whether in city or country. Farming in these days is not "easy living," but a highly skilled profession, requiring much knowledge, and actual manual labour and plenty of it. So many come to the country too light-heartedly, buy too much land, attempt unfamiliar crops, expect to hire the work done--and soon find themselves facing discouragement and failure. Any city man who would venture on this new way of life should try it first for a year or so before he commits himself--try himself out against the actual problems. Or, by moving to the country, still within reach of his accustomed work, he can have a garden or even a small farm to experiment with. The shorter work-day has made this possible for a multitude of wage-workers, and I know many instances in which life because of this opportunity to get to the soil has become a very different and much finer thing for them.

It is easy also for many men who are engaged in professional work to live where they can get their hands into the soil for part of the time at least: and this may be made as real an experience as far as it goes as though they owned wider acres and devoted their whole time to the work.

A man who thus faces the problem squarely will soon see whether country life is the thing for him; if he finds it truly so, he can be as nearly assured of "living happily ever after" as any one outside of a story-book can ever be. Out of it all is likely to come some of the greatest rewards that men can know, a robust body, a healthy appetite, a serene and cheerful spirit!

And finally there is one advantage not so easy to express. Long ago I read a story of Tolstoi's called "The Candle"--how a peasant Russian forced to plough on Easter Day lighted a candle to his Lord and kept it burning on his plough as he worked through the sacred day. When I see a man ploughing in his fields I often think of Tolstoi's peasant, and wonder if this is not as true a way as any of worshipping God. I wonder if any one truly worships God who sets about it with deliberation, or knows quite why he does it.

"My doctrine shall drop as the rain, my speech shall distil as the dew, as the small rain upon the tender herb, and as showers upon the grass."

The Codes Of Hammurabi And Moses
W. W. Davies

The discovery of the Hammurabi Code is one of the greatest achievements of archaeology, and is of paramount interest, not only to the student of the Bible, but also to all those interested in ancient history...

Religion   **ISBN: *1-59462-338-4***   **Pages:132**

QTY

MSRP $12.95

The Theory of Moral Sentiments
Adam Smith

This work from 1749. contains original theories of conscience amd moral judgment and it is the foundation for systemof morals.

Philosophy   **ISBN: *1-59462-777-0***   **Pages:536**

QTY

MSRP $19.95

Jessica's First Prayer
Hesba Stretton

In a screened and secluded corner of one of the many railway-bridges which span the streets of London there could be seen a few years ago, from five o'clock every morning until half past eight, a tidily set-out coffee-stall, consisting of a trestle and board, upon which stood two large tin cans, with a small fire of charcoal burning under each so as to keep the coffee boiling during the early hours of the morning when the work-people were thronging into the city on their way to their daily toil...

Pages:84

QTY

Childrens   **ISBN: *1-59462-373-2***   *MSRP $9.95*

My Life and Work
Henry Ford

Henry Ford revolutionized the world with his implementation of mass production for the Model T automobile. Gain valuable business insight into his life and work with his own auto-biography... "We have only started on our development of our country we have not as yet, with all our talk of wonderful progress, done more than scratch the surface. The progress has been wonderful enough but..."

Pages:300

QTY

Biographies/   **ISBN: *1-59462-198-5***   *MSRP $21.95*

The Art of Cross-Examination
Francis Wellman

I presume it is the experience of every author, after his first book is published upon an important subject, to be almost overwhelmed with a wealth of ideas and illustrations which could readily have been included in his book, and which to his own mind, at least, seem to make a second edition inevitable. Such certainly was the case with me; and when the first edition had reached its sixth impression in five months, I rejoiced to learn that it seemed to my publishers that the book had met with a sufficiently favorable reception to justify a second and considerably enlarged edition. ...

Pages:412

Reference   **ISBN:** *1-59462-647-2*   *MSRP $19.95*

QTY

On the Duty of Civil Disobedience
Henry David Thoreau

Thoreau wrote his famous essay, On the Duty of Civil Disobedience, as a protest against an unjust but popular war and the immoral but popular institution of slave-owning. He did more than write—he declined to pay his taxes, and was hauled off to gaol in consequence. Who can say how much this refusal of his hastened the end of the war and of slavery ?

Law   **ISBN:** *1-59462-747-9*   **Pages:48**

MSRP $7.45

QTY

Dream Psychology Psychoanalysis for Beginners
Sigmund Freud

Sigmund Freud, born Sigismund Schlomo Freud (May 6, 1856 - September 23, 1939), was a Jewish-Austrian neurologist and psychiatrist who co-founded the psychoanalytic school of psychology. Freud is best known for his theories of the unconscious mind, especially involving the mechanism of repression; his redefinition of sexual desire as mobile and directed towards a wide variety of objects; and his therapeutic techniques, especially his understanding of transference in the therapeutic relationship and the presumed value of dreams as sources of insight into unconscious desires.

Psychology   **ISBN:** *1-59462-905-6*   **Pages:196**

MSRP $15.45

QTY

Dream Psychology
Psychoanalysis for Beginners

Sigmund Freud

The Miracle of Right Thought
Orison Swett Marden

Believe with all of your heart that you will do what you were made to do. When the mind has once formed the habit of holding cheerful, happy, prosperous pictures, it will not be easy to form the opposite habit. It does not matter how improbable or how far away this realization may see, or how dark the prospects may be, if we visualize them as best we can, as vividly as possible, hold tenaciously to them and vigorously struggle to attain them, they will gradually become actualized, realized in the life. But a desire, a longing without endeavor, a yearning abandoned or held indifferently will vanish without realization.

Pages:360

Self Help   **ISBN:** *1-59462-644-8*   *MSRP $25.45*

QTY

www.bookjungle.com *email: sales@bookjungle.com fax: 630-214-0564 mail: Book Jungle PO Box 2226 Champaign, IL 61825*

QTY

The Rosicrucian Cosmo-Conception Mystic Christianity by *Max Heindel*   ISBN: *1-59462-188-8* **$38.95**
The Rosicrucian Cosmo-conception is not dogmatic, neither does it appeal to any other authority than the reason of the student. It is: not controversial, but is: sent forth in the, hope that it may help to clear...   New Age/Religion Pages 646

Abandonment To Divine Providence by *Jean-Pierre de Caussade*   ISBN: *1-59462-228-0* **$25.95**
"The Rev. Jean Pierre de Caussade was one of the most remarkable spiritual writers of the Society of Jesus in France in the 18th Century. His death took place at Toulouse in 1751. His works have gone through many editions and have been republished...   Inspirational/Religion Pages 400

Mental Chemistry by *Charles Haanel*   ISBN: *1-59462-192-6* **$23.95**
Mental Chemistry allows the change of material conditions by combining and appropriately utilizing the power of the mind. Much like applied chemistry creates something new and unique out of careful combinations of chemicals the mastery of mental chemistry...   New Age Pages 354

The Letters of Robert Browning and Elizabeth Barret Barrett 1845-1846 vol II   ISBN: *1-59462-193-4* **$35.95**
by *Robert Browning* and *Elizabeth Barrett*   Biographies Pages 596

Gleanings In Genesis (volume I) by *Arthur W. Pink*   ISBN: *1-59462-130-6* **$27.45**
Appropriately has Genesis been termed "the seed plot of the Bible" for in it we have, in germ form, almost all of the great doctrines which are afterwards fully developed in the books of Scripture which follow...   Religion/Inspirational Pages 420

The Master Key by *L. W. de Laurence*   ISBN: *1-59462-001-6* **$30.95**
In no branch of human knowledge has there been a more lively increase of the spirit of research during the past few years than in the study of Psychology, Concentration and Mental Discipline. The requests for authentic lessons in Thought Control, Mental Discipline and...   New Age Pages 422

The Lesser Key Of Solomon Goetia by *L. W. de Laurence*   ISBN: *1-59462-092-X* **$9.95**
This translation of the first book of the "Lernegton" which is now for the first time made accessible to students of Talismanic Magic was done, after careful collation and edition, from numerous Ancient Manuscripts in Hebrew, Latin, and French...   New Age/Occult Pages 92

Rubaiyat Of Omar Khayyam by *Edward Fitzgerald*   ISBN:*1-59462-332-5* **$13.95**
Edward Fitzgerald, whom the world has already learned, in spite of his own efforts to remain within the shadow of anonymity, to look upon as one of the rarest poets of the century, was born at Bredfield, in Suffolk, on the 31st of March, 1809. He was the third son of John Purcell...   Music Pages 172

Ancient Law by *Henry Maine*   ISBN: *1-59462-128-4* **$29.95**
The chief object of the following pages is to indicate some of the earliest ideas of mankind, as they are reflected in Ancient Law, and to point out the relation of those ideas to modern thought.   Religion/History Pages 452

Far-Away Stories by *William J. Locke*   ISBN: *1-59462-129-2* **$19.45**
"Good wine needs no bush', but a collection of mixed vintages does. And this book is just such a collection. Some of the stories I do not want to remain buried for ever in the museum files of dead magazine-numbers an author's not unpardonable vanity..."   Fiction Pages 272

Life of David Crockett by *David Crockett*   ISBN: *1-59462-250-7* **$27.45**
"Colonel David Crockett was one of the most remarkable men of the times in which he lived. Born in humble life, but gifted with a strong will, an indomitable courage, and unremitting perseverance...   Biographies/New Age Pages 424

Lip-Reading by *Edward Nitchie*   ISBN: *1-59462-206-X* **$25.95**
Edward B. Nitchie, founder of the New York School for the Hard of Hearing, now the Nitchie School of Lip-Reading, Inc, wrote "LIP-READING Principles and Practice". The development and perfecting of this meritorious work on lip-reading was an undertaking...   How-to Pages 400

A Handbook of Suggestive Therapeutics, Applied Hypnotism, Psychic Science   ISBN: *1-59462-214-0* **$24.95**
by *Henry Munro*   Health/New Age/Health/Self-help Pages 376

A Doll's House: and Two Other Plays by *Henrik Ibsen*   ISBN: *1-59462-112-8* **$19.95**
Henrik Ibsen created this classic when in revolutionary 1848 Rome. Introducing some striking concepts in playwriting for the realist genre, this play has been studied the world over.   Fiction/Classics/Plays 308

The Light of Asia by *sir Edwin Arnold*   ISBN: *1-59462-204-3* **$13.95**
In this poetic masterpiece, Edwin Arnold describes the life and teachings of Buddha. The man who was to become known as Buddha to the world was born as Prince Gautama of India but he rejected the worldly riches and abandoned the reigns of power when...   Religion/History/Biographies Pages 170

The Complete Works of Guy de Maupassant by *Guy de Maupassant*   ISBN: *1-59462-157-8* **$16.95**
"For days and days, nights and nights, I had dreamed of that first kiss which was to consecrate our engagement, and I knew not on what spot I should put my lips..."   Fiction/Classics Pages 240

The Art of Cross-Examination by *Francis L. Wellman*   ISBN: *1-59462-309-0* **$26.95**
Written by a renowned trial lawyer, Wellman imparts his experience and uses case studies to explain how to use psychology to extract desired information through questioning.   How-to/Science/Reference Pages 408

Answered or Unanswered? by *Louisa Vaughan*   ISBN: *1-59462-248-5* **$10.95**
Miracles of Faith in China   Religion Pages 112

The Edinburgh Lectures on Mental Science (1909) by *Thomas*   ISBN: *1-59462-008-3* **$11.95**
This book contains the substance of a course of lectures recently given by the writer in the Queen Street Hail, Edinburgh. Its purpose is to indicate the Natural Principles governing the relation between Mental Action and Material Conditions...   New Age/Psychology Pages 148

Ayesha by *H. Rider Haggard*   ISBN: *1-59462-301-5* **$24.95**
Verily and indeed it is the unexpected that happens! Probably if there was one person upon the earth from whom the Editor of this, and of a certain previous history, did not expect to hear again...   Classics Pages 380

Ayala's Angel by *Anthony Trollope*   ISBN: *1-59462-352-X* **$29.95**
The two girls were both pretty, but Lucy who was twenty-one who supposed to be simple and comparatively unattractive, whereas Ayala was credited, as her Bombwhat romantic name might show, with poetic charm and a taste for romance. Ayala when her father died was nineteen...   Fiction Pages 484

The American Commonwealth by *James Bryce*   ISBN: *1-59462-286-8* **$34.45**
An interpretation of American democratic political theory. It examines political mechanics and society from the perspective of Scotsman James Bryce   Politics Pages 572

Stories of the Pilgrims by *Margaret P. Pumphrey*   ISBN: *1-59462-116-0* **$17.95**
This book explores pilgrims religious oppression in England as well as their escape to Holland and eventual crossing to America on the Mayflower, and their early days in New England...   History Pages 268

QTY

The Fasting Cure *by Sinclair Upton*   ISBN: *1-59462-222-1*   **$13.95**
In the Cosmopolitan Magazine for May, 1910, and in the Contemporary Review (London) for April, 1910, I published an article dealing with my experi-ences in fasting. I have written a great many magazine articles, but never one which attracted so much attention... New Age/Self Help/Health Pages 164

Hebrew Astrology *by Sepharial*   ISBN: *1-59462-308-2*   **$13.45**
In these days of advanced thinking it is a matter of common observation that we have left many of the old landmarks behind and that we are now pressing forward to greater heights and to a wider horizon than that which represented the mind-content of our progenitors... Astrology Pages 144

Thought Vibration or The Law of Attraction in the Thought World   ISBN: *1-59462-127-6*   **$12.95**
by William Walker Atkinson   Psychology/Religion Pages 144

Optimism *by Helen Keller*   ISBN: *1-59462-108-X*   **$15.95**
Helen Keller was blind, deaf, and mute since 19 months old, yet famously learned how to overcome these handicaps, communicate with the world, and spread her lectures promoting optimism. An inspiring read for everyone... Biographies/Inspirational Pages 84

Sara Crewe *by Frances Burnett*   ISBN: *1-59462-360-0*   **$9.45**
In the first place, Miss Minchin lived in London. Her home was a large, dull, tall one, in a large, dull square, where all the houses were alike, and all the sparrows were alike, and where all the door-knockers made the same heavy sound... Childrens/Classic Pages 88

The Autobiography of Benjamin Franklin *by Benjamin Franklin*   ISBN: *1-59462-135-7*   **$24.95**
The Autobiography of Benjamin Franklin has probably been more extensively read than any other American historical work, and no other book of its kind has had such ups and downs of fortune. Franklin lived for many years in England, where he was agent... Biographies/History Pages 332

Name	
Email	
Telephone	
Address	
City, State ZIP	

☐ **Credit Card**   ☐ **Check / Money Order**

Credit Card Number	
Expiration Date	
Signature	

Please Mail to: Book Jungle
PO Box 2226
Champaign, IL 61825
or Fax to: 630-214-0564

www.ingramcontent.com/pod-product-compliance
Lightning Source LLC
Chambersburg PA
CBHW082014170626
46817CB00009B/3090